Louis Evan Shipman

D'Arcy of the Guards

Or, the fortunes of war

Louis Evan Shipman

D'Arcy of the Guards
Or, the fortunes of war

ISBN/EAN: 9783337272258

Printed in Europe, USA, Canada, Australia, Japan

Cover: Foto ©Andreas Hilbeck / pixelio.de

More available books at **www.hansebooks.com**

D'ARCY *of the* GUARDS

OR

The FORTUNES *of* WAR

D'ARCY *of the* GUARDS

OR

The FORTUNES *of* WAR

BY

LOUIS EVAN SHIPMAN

HERBERT S. STONE *and Company*

CHICAGO *and* NEW YORK

MDCCCXCIX

NICHOLAS BIDDLE

My dear Nic: You and I have shared
in common, so wide and various an
acquaintance, and have allowed our
disfancies and admirations to go so often
hand in hand, that I feel some hesitancy
in commending Major John Gerald
D'Arcy—D'Arcy of the Guards—to your
special consideration. You will not find
him worthy of the little company which
includes our old intimates, the Marquis
of Esmond, James Durie, David Bal-
four, Richard Feverel, Richmond Roy
and Christopher Newman, but the fault
of that belongs to me. And if he does
take some small place in your affection,
I am content enough to think that it
will not be for his sake, but for mine.

Your friend,

New York   LOUIS EVAN SHIPMAN

February, 1899

CONTENTS

D'Arcy *of the* Guards

CHAPTER I

THE INN ON THE HEATH

It was a black night near the end of March in the year 1777, and on that very blackness depended the fate of a gallant officer in His Majesty's service, of a certain maid far away in His Majesty's rebellious American colonies, and the telling of this tale; so often do we find the most momentous instant in our lives hang by the slender thread of a seeming unimportant circumstance. For if the sluggard moon had not been held back beyond his usual wont by a band of riotous and surly clouds, Dick Conyngham and his pals would never have ventured on so hazardous an undertaking; Major D'Arcy would never have been able to put the Marquis of G—— under an obligation; and that omnipotent nobleman would never have

1

lifted a finger for the betterment of the young soldier's military fortunes, which hung very slack just at this time, as we shall presently see.

On the edge of the heath not half a score of miles from London, and back from the highway less than a good stone's throw, stood the "Jolly George," a humble but cheerful hostelry, that was particularly affected by Mr. Richard Conyngham and his select circle of night-riders; as audacious and dashing a body of toll-gatherers as ever wore mask and infested the king's post-roads. The casual wayfarer seldom passed into its sanded tap-room; not on account of any prejudice against the hospitality offered there, but because the inn itself was scarce visible from the main road, either by night or day. So its chief visitors were made up of post-boys, coachmen, postillions: the riffraff of the road, and the initiated few of Mr. Conyngham's profession, for whom was reserved the little parlor one step down and back from the tap-room.

It was in special requisition this night,

2

and no less a person than Dick Conyngham himself leaned over the fire poking moodily at the blazing embers. His companions, Gerdor, an able lieutenant of Conyngham's, and Jemmy Twill, the landlord, a twinkle-eyed rogue, hand-in-glove with these light-fingered gentry, puffed spasmodically at their church - wardens, and were visibly depressed by the moody man's low spirits.

"I tell you what's truth, Gerdor," he said at last, straightening himself after a last vicious lunge with the tongs, "if we don't make a decent haul in the next three nights, I'm for the North Road."

"As you say, Captain," replied Gerdor.

"But what am *I* to do?" asked Twill, his glass of spirits suspended between lips and table.

"Oh, you be damned," answered Conyngham, turning a black face toward him. "You're the only one in the crowd that makes anything, and you risk nothing."

"Very kindly spoke, Dick Conyngham. But memory should serve you better."

"Oh, shut up, Jemmy," flung out

3

Gerdor through a rift of smoke. But Jemmy didn't; he opened wide, drained his glass and, evidently finding conciliation at the bottom of it, whipped his temper about. "What's the use of complaining, Dick; you've done well enough," he said.

"What d'ye call 'well enough'? A beggarly handful of guineas, and my lodging paid? I tell you," turning once more to Gerdor, "we've got to change."

"I feel it in my bones that our luck is on the mend, Dick," said Gerdor.

"It could mend much and gain us little," said the other, rising and propping the mantel-shelf with his great shoulders.

"Wait till Kit turns up; he may have good news this very night," put in Twill.

"I tell you, we've wrung the road dry, and what if the coach has anything to-night? The cursed moon has turned night into day, and the country's as bright as the Mall at noon."

"Don't be so sure of that, Captain," said Gerdor. "I have an idea that Oliver has had his eyes closed for the night." He rose and pushed back the curtains.

4

"I'd stake my life on it, now," he added. "It's as black a night as I ever could wish for."

Conyngham stepped to his side and cast a weather-wise eye at the quickly-moving masses of black cloud that told of the coming storm.

"Well?" questioned Twill.

"A splendid night for an empty coach," was all the reply he got, as Conyngham lazily dropped into a chair.

"I'll bet you five quid, Dick, that we bag a full purse to-night," Gerdor said, turning from the window, his spirits revived by the outside gloom.

"Done," said Conyngham. "If you win, you're welcome to them; if I win, they'll be welcome to me."

"And what time can we expect Kit, Jemmy?" asked Gerdor.

"He was to wait at Demford for the coach; if it was anything worth while, he would be back here by nine, if not he would take his time."

"It is now nine, less ten minutes," said Conyngham, raising his eyes to the little clock that was furiously ticking out

5

its race against time. "If he's not here in twenty minutes, I win."

"You don't win till break of dawn," laughed Gerdor. "Purses have been lifted between the hours of ten at night and six in the morning."

"Optimism has been the death of better men than you, Gerdor," sneered his chief.

"Well, I say some more spirits," suggested Twill, and meeting with no remonstrance, he bustled into the tap-room, and replenished the glasses.

Gerdor, roused from his previous apathy, was now impatiently pacing the room; now stopping at the window; now facing the clock with screwed brows. For the hand was already past the hour, and the tip of a smile was beginning to hover around Conyngham's thin lips.

Jemmy had returned, and he and Gerdor drank the perennial toast of all highwaymen, in all times: a full purse, to the sarcastic accompaniment of Conyngham's "Some other night on some other road."

- "I believe you'd let a Bishop slip through your fingers to-night, Dick, just to win my miserable five quid, and to be able to crack one of your miserable jokes," said Gerdor.

"On the contrary, I'll fight a coach load to help you win; I hope to God you will—for my own sake."

"It's getting late for Kit," remarked Twill, comparing his watch with the ticker on the shelf.

"Damn the luck," muttered Gerdor.

"Thank you," said Conyngham, and he smiled in an abstracted way, as he balanced the blade of his sword on one hand.

Gerdor's moment of enthusiasm seemed to have passed; he drew a chair, in no good humor, to the table, and mechanically examined the priming of two neat-looking pistols, while Twill remained the only sanguine member of the trio, with still an eye for the clock, and an ear for the noises of the night outside.

It was the alert Conyngham, though, that first caught the sound of an approaching horseman at full gallop. Listlessness dropped from him like a flash, and his black eyes sparkled with the light of anticipation, as he stepped quickly to the door at the side, which opened on the tiny courtyard, and flung it open. Gerdor and Twill were at his back in a second.

"What is it, Dick?" asked Gerdor.

"Kit," answered Conyngham, "and he has some news worth the telling, or he's using the spur for nothing."

"You're right, he's coming on at a pace," exclaimed Twill, as he held a flickering candle high overhead, and peered out into the black.

By this time the rider had turned from the road into the lane, and was making straight for the inn. Evidently the shimmer of Twill's candle-light had become visible, for a loud "Halloa" came out of the darkness.

"It is Dick," ejaculated Gerdor, and Conyngham gave an answering shout. A second later Kit Darrell and his steaming mare pulled up before the three expectant worthies. A peculiar whistle from Twill brought a sleepy hostler out of the stables, who, after an admonition from Darrell, led away the fagged mount, and the group pushed back into the parlor.

8

"News, Kit?" asked Conyngham, sharply.

"The best."

"Out with it, then," said Gerdor, scarce able to conceal his impatience.

"The coach leaves Demford at nine," said Darrell, addressing himself to Conyngham.

"Yes, go on."

"With two passengers."

"Is that all?" interrupted Twill.

"Shut up, Twill. Go on Kit," said Conyngham, angrily.

"One of 'em is a Major D'Arcy, the other is some government nob, and we ought to get six hundred guineas between 'em."

"Who is on the box?" questioned Gerdor.

"Bill Mace."

"Good," remarked Conyngham. "And who is the guard?"

"A new one," said Kit, "we'll have to finish him."

"Easy enough," rejoined the Captain.

"Is D'Arcy armed, and the other one?"

"Yes. I tried to get at their pistols at

9

Demford, but the blackguards took 'em into supper with them."

"I hate suspicious passengers," remarked Twill.

"Where's the best place to do the business?" asked Gerdor.

"There's only one place," answered Conyngham, "in the hollow by the bridge. We must be off in five minutes. A glass of brandy, all around, Jemmy."

"Right you are, Dick," said Twill, as he hurried up the step into the bar.

"Take a look at your pistols, boys. Fresh priming won't go amiss," ordered Conyngham, the note of command coming into his voice. And by the time Jemmy returned with the refreshment, three pair of murderous-looking pistols had been freshly primed, cloaks and hats had been donned, spurs tightened and swords adjusted. The old toast was drunk with gusto, and the three issued to the yard ready for their adventure, the dancing light of Twill's lantern throwing giant shadows as they strode forward.

A moment later they were in the saddle, and with a wave to Twill swept gallantly

down the lane, to meet what was to be
the most serious event in Mr. Richard
Conyngham's life. Twill stood gazing
after, till the night swallowed them, and
the last pounding of hoofs sounded in his
ear.

CHAPTER II

It was shortly before noon of the same day, whose later course saw the adventurers depart from the inn on the heath, that the London coach, Bill Mace on the box, drew up in the yard of the "Bush Tree" at Belden, and deposited a solitary passenger on the doorstep. This gentleman's descent from the vehicle was watched with close, quick scrutiny from behind a curtained window, and his appearance warranted the hasty and obsequious attention of the landlord at the portal of his house, where he bent his lowest, as Major D'Arcy passed into the ordinary. The degree of genuflection is a sure determinant of mine host's opinion, and there was nothing doubtful in the impression which the young soldier made on the worthy hostelkeeper, who now hurried after him to do the utmost courtesy of kitchen and cellar.

13

And in truth John Gerald D'Arcy was a man who left impressions, the most definite, on all whom he chanced to meet. The eyes that looked straight; the mouth that held firm, or relaxed in gaiety or to mock; the nose that told of birth, all made for a face of singular strength and sensibility; while the lithe, strong body spoke quietly of the graces that nature and fashion give but to a fortunate few. He stood for a moment, ungloved, with outstretched hands before the huge fire of crackling chestnut, that vied eagerly with streaming sunshine, to heat the comfortable room, then made his way to a corner table and ordered plentifully: meat of the land—beef, in quantity, with a dusty bottle from across the channel to keep it company; he named it with no uncertainty, loading thereby, with chains, the admiration of his host, who waited. This done, he demanded the "London Gazette" of latest date, and was soon skipping its columns for news of the army. With not much satisfaction to himself, however, as the result, and he cast the sheet impatiently aside, and drummed

aimlessly on the table, while his brows were
screwed perplexedly.

He was just recovering from a painful
wound in the leg, received most gallantly
in the affray with the American rebels at
White Plains, New York, six months
before, and yet, with a record that hardly
another officer in the Guards could equal,
his career in the army—near the dearest
thing in the world to him—was brought
to a full stop, and he had a lively prevision
of its absolute curtailment, which calls
for short retrospect and a small matter of
personal history.   He was the only son of
one of those anomalies, a rich Irish peer,
Lord D'Arcy, himself a soldier bred, and
tried, as a flapping, armless sleeve betok-
ened; mute evidence of the day at Minden
years before.   The tradition of the
D'Arcys included at least three terms at
Trinity College, Dublin; tradition, however, could only force young Jack, rebellious and reluctant, through two, when his
father gave up the fight and packed him
off to Paris as secretary on the Embassy,
where he stayed for three years, acquiring
many choice accomplishments, including

several unusual tricks with the rapier, his skill with which was phenomenal, and a pretty taste in lace and shoebuckles. His experience was a valuable one, nevertheless, and so impressed his father that when a change of ministry brought the youngster back to London, the old soldier presented him with a captaincy in the Guards, where, though but a stripling of six and twenty, he took place immediately. Not, I confess, was it firmly established, however, till he had the young Marquis of Vane out one fine morning, for some flippant comment on the style of his hair. He was perfectly satisfied with disarming his older antagonist, and his hair became the fashion. So did its wearer. He was an idol of the town. No rout was quite successful without him, and no fête, breakfast or supper. No one lost at hazard with quite so good a grace; and no one held rapier or pressed trigger with firmer hand. Coffee-house and club flung open welcome doors at his approach, and the Guards' mess with him to give the toasts was a thing of joy; while the old lord looked on and grew young again, pay-ing guineas by the thousand for privilege; and Lady D'Arcy, a simple lady who hated the mad, unnatural London life, watched it all with faltering heart and misgivings for her boy.

But the years slipped by, and he was the same simple, lovable Jack D'Arcy. Dissipation laid a light hand on him, and common sense took hold. He was still a town gallant, but his gaiety was more subdued. An affair with Lady Betty Kew—more serious than a score of previous ones, and necessitating constant journeyings and almost removal to Bath—had a sobering influence, that was rather intensified when the inconstant jilted him for the Earl of Strathleigh, who carried his arm in a sling for some months afterwards, however, as the result of her indiscretion. It was about this time that he got his majority; and command of a battalion added to the seemliness of his port, though it took nothing from his good humor, and his brogue lost none of its insinuating charm.

Then came parlous days. The rabble in the American colonies were becoming defiant, seditious, even rebellious, and the Guards were shipped off to Boston Harbor, to teach the provincials a needed lesson in loyalty and obedience, which curiously enough they refused to learn. And one fine day Jack D'Arcy, at the head of his battalion, charged up Breed's Hill to scatter the intrenched and fool-hardy yokels. But—that any one should live to chronicle it—the Guards scattered and fled before they reached the top, with Jack and his brother officers cursing and belaboring their backs with their swords. They reformed at the bottom and undertook the hideous task again, with like result; once more and this time with success, but with what a tale to tell at muster call! D'Arcy was complimented by Sir William Howe, and, twinkling, remarked that "the hill must have been defended by Irishmen." It might as well not have been taken at all, as it turned out, for the inconsiderate Mr. Washington, not long after, forced the whole British army to retire, and it set sail for New York, where fell the mischance that was like to bring ill-fame to the house of D'Arcy and disaster to its heir.

It was this: among the group of young officers that served on the staff of General Howe was a certain young nobleman whose father was a younger brother of the powerful Marquis of G——. He, in common with most of his associates, among whom was D'Arcy, spent most of his nights at the gaming table. And after the Battle of Long Island (where His Majesty's forces, with some slight aid from their German allies, literally annihilated the Colonials, and which put the pleasant town of New York completely at their disposal), the gambling was high and incessant. One night—it was a memorable one to D'Arcy—this young nobleman was pitted against the Guardsman for hours, and arose livid from the sitting, a temporary bankrupt. But, taking his ill-luck unkindly, he dashed the cards in his rival's face, with a foul insinuation. The provocation was flagrant, the insult heard by a room full that jumped to its feet aghast. Apology was demanded and refused; the insult repeated, and they

19

met not half an hour afterward. The young nobleman was grievously wounded, and try never so hard as the participants did, the affair could not be hushed up, and came to the ears of Headquarters, where dueling was frowned at and stamped upon viciously. Luckily for Major D'Arcy, the fight at White Plains occurred two days afterward, and he fell with a bullet in his leg, which enabled Headquarters to be lenient, and he was gazetted home on sick leave (on the same ship, in fact, that carried the wounded young nobleman), with private advices, however, for the war office, to the effect that he had better not again be given active service!

In ignorance of this, once convalescence was past, he made application for immediate detail on active duty, but to his astonishment and chagrin, he was placed only on waiting orders. For two months now, he and his father had been bringing every influence to bear, leaving no stone unturned, to get orders returning him to his regiment in the colonies. To no purpose. The young nobleman's friends, among whom was the powerful Marquis of G——, before spoken of, who fed in the matter a private grudge of years' standing against Lord D'Arcy, foiled their every attempt, and the house of D'Arcy was in despair.

Day after day the "Gazette" appeared, with always the same hideous omission: no orders for Major John Gerald D'Arcy, of the Grenadier Guards. The town began to talk. Why, if Major D'Arcy was so brilliant an officer, did Government detain him in London? was a question on tip-tongue of the malignant, and one difficult of answer by the old Lord's intimates and the Guardsman's friends. It took credulity the most amiable to believe that the people of the wounded young nobleman were using such strenuous efforts to ruin the career of his opponent. Yet such was the case. Their success, too, was assured with the powerful aid of the Marquis of G——, and they would have continued to baffle every move on D'Arcy's part, if Chance had not taken pity on his quandary and presented, all unknown to him, a solution.

He had finished his meal and paid the

account. A glimpse through the window of fresh horses being put to the coach, gave notice that the start was at hand. His fingers were at the buckle of his cloak, when his host stood before him, hesitating and embarrassed, but with evident import in his manner.

"Pardon me, sir, but you've booked the whole coach for London, sir, have you not?" was his question.

"I have."

"I beg pardon, sir, but there is a gentleman——"

"I know," interrupted D'Arcy, "but the gentleman will not get to London to-night—in my coach. If I preferred company I should not have booked all the seats."

"I quite understand, sir," stammered the landlord, "but the gentleman's private chariot has broken down just beyond the town, and it is most important that he should reach London to-night."

"Why doesn't he hire a chaise?"

"There are but two in the town, sir, and they are engaged."

"What did you say was the gentleman's

name?'' questioned D'Arcy, relenting a trifle.

"Mr.—Mr. Blunt," quavered Boniface, feeling, however, that he had gained his point, which he had.

"And can you vouch for him?" asked D'Arcy. "I've no desire to ride up to London with some light-fingered gentleman who may take a fancy to my watches."

"Oh, sir," cried the man, almost hysterically, as D'Arcy remembered afterward, "that the likes of me should ever dare to give the likes of him a character!"

"Well, tell your Mr. Blunt to look sharp," laughed D'Arcy, convinced that his fellow traveler would not disturb the peace, and he made exit to the courtyard in time to hear Mace, the ruddy Jehu, giving final directions about the off leader, while the guard was shoving the last parcels into the apron. A few moments later, he was aware of some one coming out behind him, and wheeling about, he came face to face with a tall, vigorous, distinguished looking, old gentleman, whose eyes seemed to bore through every-

23

thing they lighted on. The inn keeper followed humbly at his heels, and carried two leather portmanteaux.

"I imagine, sir, that it is to your courtesy I am indebted for my coach-seat," said the gentleman, addressing D'Arcy.

"Is this—a—Mr.—Mr. Blunt?" questioned D'Arcy, staring. He had prefigured to himself some dapper goldsmith or smug and comfortable draper, and was entirely unprepared for the man of undoubted fashion and breeding who addressed him.

"Yes," was the reply, "I am the Mr. Blunt whom the good man here has recommended to your consideration."

"The pleasure is mine, sir," announced D'Arcy.

"And may I ask the name of the gentleman by whose condescension I ride? You are of the army, sir?" questioned Blunt, taking in the military cloak, and the gleam of scarlet coat that showed from under.

"Major D'Arcy——"

"Not D'Arcy of the Guards?" asked

the old man quickly, and his eyes fairly snapped, as he waited for reply.

"The same," said D'Arcy, not unpleased at the other's knowledge. "Have we friends in common?"

"I think not," said the other, icily, and turned to give directions for the bestowal of his bags, which being accomplished, he entered the coach, followed by D'Arcy, much to the relief of Mace, who, as the nimble guard slammed the door, gave the leaders their head, the wheelers his whip, and the coach plunged out of the yard; the huzzas of the hostlers sounding after far down the road.

CHAPTER III

The scent of earth hung on the afternoon air—first token of a laggard spring; the sun—old-time peacemaker between the seasons—stood high at first, forcing the last bit of reluctant frost from out the ground (innocent cause of Mace's anathemas, as he urged his steaming horses on, while first front, then back wheels sunk, hub-deep, into the mire), then played hide-and-seek with some scudding clouds that spoke of a brewing storm, and finally disappeared behind the hills, leaving a chill wind to remind the travelers, in a cutting way, of his genial absence.

D'Arcy's companion had settled himself comfortably in the ample folds of a sable-lined cloak, and though taciturn and uninclined to converse, D'Arcy felt that the older man was watching him closely. He was convinced, too, that Mr. Blunt was traveling incognito: no plain *mister*

27

journeyed in furs or dipped snuff—
genuine Vigo—from a jeweled snuff-box;
and there was an air of distinction and
quality about the man that no mere "Mr.
Blunt" could have possessed. But it
worried D'Arcy not a whit, though he did
wonder why the mention of his name had
frozen the stranger's cordiality.

It was over the jeweled snuff-box that
conversation first opened. Amiably accept-
ing its polite proffer, D'Arcy drew off a
glove, and took a pinch of the aromatic
powder, commenting at the same time on
its choice flavor.

"Ah, yes," said Blunt, snapping the
box lid, and dusting his fingers delicately.
"I'll give up the habit when my stock of
this is gone. You younger men of the army
don't affect it much?" he questioned.

"We've fallen low, and smoke the
weed," laughed D'Arcy.

"A vicious use of it," remarked the
other.

"It has compensations."

"But no graces," said Blunt.

"We have not the manners of our
fathers," remarked D'Arcy.

" 'Twere better if you had."

"You grasp my meaning entirely, sir."

"The soldiers of your father's day would not have fled before a mob of farmers," said the old man, irrelevantly and with some bitterness.

"You refer to the campaign in the colonies?" asked D'Arcy

"I do, sir."

"The soldiers of my father's time were never pitted against Englishmen."

"Don't call that rabble English," cried the other, testily.

"Call 'em what you will, they fight like Englishmen," said D'Arcy.

"Well, Burgoyne will settle the business before the year is out," remarked Blunt, having recourse once more to the snuff-box.

"I trust so," answered D'Arcy, abstractedly.

"And when do you rejoin your regiment?" questioned Blunt, his eyes twinkling, unnoticed by his companion.

"God knows!" ejaculated D'Arcy. "An honorable wound seems no recommendation to Government for active service, and they keep me here eating my heart out, while they send the king's money to Germany for men who have not the slightest inclination to join in the quarrel."

"I have heard something of it," said Blunt.

"No doubt," rejoined D'Arcy.

"You need friends at court."

"It's a sorry day for soldiers when their records don't plead for 'em," said D'Arcy, drily

"Records are double-faced," ventured the old man, snuffing.

"What do you mean by that, sir?"

"Young blades nowadays are too fond of their blades," said the other, glancing out of the window, as if to attach no special significance to his words.

"Ah," said D'Arcy, in wonder; "you've heard of that affair? Well, let me tell you, sir, that when a man who holds His Majesty's commission refuses to draw his sword in defense of his honor, it will be a bad day for His Majesty."

"May be," said Blunt, curtly, and they relapsed into silence, D'Arcy cudgeling his brain for the identity of the man, who, by innuendo, showed himself so knowing his personal affairs.

The color of the afternoon had changed to gray, and at five, as they cantered down the high street of Scorley, the lights were twinkling all about, and the night was coming on apace. There was a quick change of horses, and lighting of lanterns, while Mace and the alert guard gulped their spirits in the tap-room; then, with a loud "Get along, lads," from Mace, and a merry wind from the guard's horn, they dashed out of town toward Demford, the next stop. They had almost reached that village, after three hours of temper-trying jolts, before D'Arcy again addressed his companion, who had evidently been dozing most part of the time, judging from the familiar sounds that came out of the cloak which muffled him.

"I am told my host of the Demford Inn offers very good cheer," he said, "and we are near at hand, if I've not mistaken."

"Hunger has me in its grip," murmured Blunt, sitting up. "What's the hour?"

D'Arcy tugged at his fob, and the repeater chimed eight and the quarter.

"Good," said the old man, "almost on time."

"If these cursed roads were not so hellish rough," said D'Arcy, "we would be in London by two."

"It's a sad journey for gouty legs," remarked Blunt.

"It's a miserable journey for any," rejoined D'Arcy. And at that moment, with a loud clatter the horses struck the cobbles of the inn yard, and with a hearty "Who-a!" Mace brought them up on their haunches, just beyond the wide-open door.

Several aproned drawers from the tap-room, headed by the beaming host, whose jaw fell when two only descended from the coach, but whose face resumed its wonted smile again when he became aware of their quality, bustled about and assisted the stiffened passengers into the lighted, cheery ordinary, where a welcome blaze of logs, made particularly bitter, by comparison, the remembrance of their dreary hour's ride.

A supper was ordered that fully justified

the landlord in his opinion of his guests, and they ate ravenously, not slighting either what they drank. In fact, Blunt engulfed such prodigious quantities of port that his gout was no longer a mystery —if it ever was—to his younger companion. He mellowed, too, under its potency, and leaned to D'Arcy with laughing eyes better to catch the fun of the Irishman's wit, which was bubbling. So loud they grew, and really gay, that the clock's hands fairly flew in disgust at their ribaldry, and stood pointing at the hour of departure—nine, before they were aware.

"Is the road clear?" asked D'Arcy of the keeper, as they stood once more on the threshold.

"There have been one or two suspicious characters about the town these last two days, sir," replied the man.

"No robberies, though?"

"None for a week past, sir."

"This is Conyngham's borough, isn't it?" said Blunt.

"He is supposed to be about, sir," answered the landlord.

"Then it's a rotten one," laughed

D'Arcy. "Come on, Mr. Blunt, we'll risk Conyngham."

Blunt followed the Irishman rather dubiously, and was particular in the rearrangement of his portmanteaux. They were fixed at last, however, and the start made.

"Have you pistols, Major?" asked Blunt.

"I have, Mr. Blunt, and a pretty pair of barkers they are." He leaned forward and drew two silver-mounted pistols from his capacious pockets. "I'll just look to their priming. May you happen to have anything of the sort yourself?"

"Yes, here," replied Blunt.

"And your rapier?" questioned D'Arcy.

"Yes," said Blunt.

"Fie, fie, Mr. Blunt, you should leave blades to the blades, sir."

"You have me there, Major," laughed Blunt.

"Well, you'll admit they're handy weapons on occasion."

"You're better authority than I," said the old man, in the same tone that had stopped conversation before.

"Well, I won't deny it," said D'Arcy, "and I entirely agree with my own opinion."

"It's as black as the ace of spades," remarked the old man, peering out.

"It's as black as the deuce of spades, which is just twice as black as the ace," rejoined D'Arcy, leaning to his window.

"Well, it must be endured," he added, settling himself as comfortably as was possible in the swaying, lurching chariot, while Blunt did the same.

They had struggled on through the night for near an hour—D'Arcy had appealed to his repeater once, and it had chimed the three-quarters—when they struck a comparatively level bit of road.

"We must be cutting across country now," remarked D'Arcy.

"Why?" questioned Blunt.

"We're running so smoothly," answered the Irishman gaily, and the words were scarce off his lips when the coach came to a stop, with a jolt that sent them flying forward. At the same moment there were two shots in quick succession and a jumble of cursing voices.

"Quick, man, your pistols!" cried D'Arcy, and he sprang from the coach, just as a giant figure charged up on horseback. "Give way there, you damned scoundrel," yelled Gerdor, with an oath. They fired simultaneously, and D'Arcy heard the crash of glass behind, while Gerdor, with a cry or a sob, faded into the black of his mount, which reared, and galloped off with a senseless thing bouncing on its rump.

There were shots on the far side of the coach, too, and then D'Arcy, as he ran forward, heard the quick click of steel. He pushed under the heads of the quivering leaders and stumbled against a man lying huddled; as he recovered himself and turned, the blood seemed driven from his heart. In the feeble shimmering light that the coach lamp cast, he saw Blunt, his old face spread over with a fearful pallor, standing with his back against the panels, in the last weak struggle with a man who seemed to be playing with him, so supple and powerful did he show in every movement. With a shout D'Arcy sprang toward them. "You bastard!" he cried, "fight with a man your equal," and he engaged with Dick Conyngham, at the very moment that Blunt's sword fell from his hand, and the old man himself sank exhausted.

"I'll slit that white throat of yours," gasped Conyngham; but in the moment of saying it he knew that he had met his master; he was fighting against a wrist of steel and a skill that was infernal. With a curse he gave ground before the fierce assault of his opponent, and the second later—so swiftly that the blackguard never knew his fate—D'Arcy's blade drove through his heart. Dick Conyngham had won his wager!

Blunt slowly crawled to his feet, and stood shaking like one with a palsy. His lips were ashen, and his eyes burned with the fever of fear. He put out an unsteady hand as D'Arcy came up. "My God, man," he mumbled, "you've saved my life."

"The rascal had a strong wrist, but he was a novice," said D'Arcy, supporting Blunt while he unscrewed a flask and put the brandy to his lips. Then he added: "It was a very pretty fight."

"Pretty fight be damned!" ejaculated the other. "It was abominable."

"As you please, sir," acquiesced D'Arcy, and he drained the remainder of the potent liquid himself. "And now let's look about us."

They found the once nimble guard sprawling forward on the top of the coach, quite dead; under the feet of the frightened leaders lay Kit Darrell; the guard had brought him down the first shot. Of Bill Mace, the driver, they could find no trace, though they beat about the road on either side for yards, and made the night echo with their halloas.

"It's a good riddance of the rascal," said Blunt, at last.

"Which means that I must tool the hearse into London," answered D'Arcy, comically. And he did, with Blunt sitting beside him on the box.

The towers of the city were toning three as they swung through the deserted streets, and the far-away cry of the watch on its round echoed "All's well!" which was right, save for the dead guard lurching backward and forward inside the coach, and Dick Conyngham and his pal lying out on the heath miles away.

As for Major John Gerald D'Arcy, the little adventure of the night, all unknown to him, had changed the current of his life.

CHAPTER IV

AN INVITATION TO SUPPER

The London sun had risen, hung high over the city, and was well on its descent before D'Arcy awoke the following day, in his father's house, and rang for his servant. That worthy appeared immediately, evidently being in wait for the summons, his face lighted with a grin of welcome.

"Tim, you rascal," cried D'Arcy, springing up, "why didn't you call me? The day's gone."

"Faith, Master Jack, I was waiting for you to call me," answered Tim, echoing his master's brogue.

"Well, get me dressed and shaved at once, ye spalpeen. Do you want me to lose a whole day out of my life?" And in a moment master and man were inextricably mixed in the mysteries of a dandy's toilet. For D'Arcy was a dandy, and few men of fashion in the town equaled him in his finery, and no valet

41

compared with Tim, to whom the chief
savor of life came from boasting, at the
coffee house and footman's club, where he
was a privileged member, of D'Arcy's
pre-eminence among the London gallants.

The operation once over, the guardsman, exquisitely powdered and patched,
and wrapped in the most gorgeous of
brocaded dressing-gowns, sipped his dish
of chocolate and fingered a pile of accumu-
lated notes, bills and letters that were
spread before him.

"Are my father and mother well,
Tim?" he asked.

"Very, sir. And his lordship and my
lady are very anxious to see you."

"Take my compliments to Lady
D'Arcy, and say that I shall pay my
respects to her in half an hour."

"Yes, sir."

He was departing on his errand, when a
tap at the door halted him.

"What is it?" questioned D'Arcy.

There was whispering through the door-
crack between a footman and Tim.

"It's Captain Gregory is below wanting
to see you, sir," said the latter.

"Tell the blockhead to show him up at once."

"Ye blockhead, show him up at once," said Tim loudly after the departing flunkey, and then he left the room with his own messages.

At the sound of footsteps along the passage, D'Arcy threw down a half-read letter and rushed to the door. There was a welcome in his eyes that shone for few, and he grasped the huge red-coated figure that entered a moment later, in a pressure of arms that made the other wince. "Greg, me boy, you're a joy to me sight," said D'Arcy.

"Unhand me, you ruffian," gasped Gregory, struggling.

"May I ask where you come from?" laughed the Irishman, holding him off at arm's length.

"You may, but you'll get no satisfaction till you answer the same question about yourself."

"Just from the hands of Tim," answered D'Arcy, sparkling.

"I can see that," sniffed Gregory, tapping his snuff-box and taking a pinch.

"You've powder enough in your hair for a battalion, and you're patched like Peg Woffington."

Gregory's own hair needed little to whiten it, and as for patches, they would have looked like milestones, on his red, wrinkled visage.

"You're a man of no taste, Captain Gregory. I refer you to Tim, if you'd know half me beauties," laughed D'Arcy.

"You're a damnable coxcomb," said the other.

"Well, you're lucky to be able to call names at me here this morning."

"What d'ye mean?" asked Gregory; "not more of your cursed folly?"

"I crossed swords with a gentleman last night," said D'Arcy.

"What!" cried Gregory.

And the story was told, with a touch of humor to relieve its ghastliness, and a listener who sat agape.

"And who was Blunt?" he asked, at the conclusion.

"A man of mystery."

"And where did he go?"

"He was met at the 'Bell and Crown,'

when we drew up, by a couple of servants and disappeared.''

''Didn't you ask who he was?'' questioned Gregory.

''I was too sleepy to care.''

''You're beautiful,'' said the captain, in querulous disgust.

''Thank you,'' laughed D'Arcy. ''I knew you'd come around.''

''It sounds like a chap-book story.''

''I'd swear it was a dream if it wasn't for this.'' And D'Arcy, taking down a cloak, showed where Gerdor's bullet had clipped its way. ''And this,'' he added, handing Gregory the stained blade.

''You saved Blunt's life,'' cried Gregory.

''And the other rascal's soul, Greg.''

''Well, you almost take the life out of my news,'' said the other.

''What is it?'' asked D'Arcy, eagerly. ''Not—not——'' he faltered, as his friend drew a paper from his coat.

''Yes, Jack, it's come at last. Read that.''

D'Arcy had eagerly grasped the ''Gazette,'' and read with breaking voice:

"Captain Charles Gregory, surgeon of the 1st battalion of Foot Guards, has been ordered on active duty to the colonies in America."

"Oh, Greg, I am glad," he cried, almost choking, "but I wish I were going too."

"I'll not go unless you do, lad," said Gregory, quietly.

"Are you mad, Greg?" said D'Arcy, staring.

"No—angry," answered the older man, sniffing huge quantities of the contents of his little box.

"My father and I can never allow it," replied D'Arcy, quickly.

"Since when have my Lord D'Arcy and Major D'Arcy assumed control of my actions?"

"Listen, Greg," said the young soldier, pleadingly.

"Listen yourself," snapped the doctor, visibly ruffled, and he went on before D'Arcy could protest further: "I have served in the British army thirty odd years. I was at Minden sixteen years ago, where your father was chief aide on Lord

Granby's staff, and I saved his life, if I couldn't save his arm, that day. You were a lad then, but you were a man later when I went to Quebec with Wolfe. For the past two years, you and I have been together, Jack, doing our best for a foolish king and his mad ministers, and now, if after all you've suffered they have no place for you at the front, they will have one more vacancy to fill; for I'll quit the service."

"You're a dear old Greg," said D'Arcy, taking his friend's hand, "but I never could allow any such sacrifice."

"Sacrifice!" ejaculated Gregory. "Why, boy, there would be no pleasure for me out there without you."

"We'll speak with my father about it. I haven't seen him yet; he may have news."

"I'm afraid not, Jack. It's about town, that the war office is down on you, and I believe it's so."

"It's not the war office. It's that cursed young beast and his cursed old protector, the Marquis of G——," said D'Arcy, angrily.

47

"You're right; they're at the bottom of it."

"Faith, I wish they were at the bottom of the pit," rejoined the young man.

"Oh, why will you mix in silly quarrels, lad?" groaned the doctor.

"And would you have had me put up with the young blackguard's insults?"

"You should have caned him."

"He needed a little blood-letting," answered D'Arcy. "I'm sorry I let him off so easily, now."

"You're your father's own son," sighed Gregory.

"You compliment my mother," laughed D'Arcy. "Come," he added, "we'll go to the old gentleman." Throwing off his gown, he adjusted his coat and ruffles before a mirror—to the scoffing of Gregory, whose own frills were of the simplest—and a few moments later they were making their way to the apartments of Lord D'Arcy.

They found the old lord in the book-room enveloped in a cloud of smoke, from which he emerged, pipe in hand, to give them a boisterous welcome.

"Ye rogues," he cried, "you're a long time reporting to your superior officer."

"The fine gentleman was at his curling irons," laughed Gregory.

"That I should ever have fathered a fop," said my lord, winking slyly at his old comrade.

"Greg says I'm my father's own son."

"And so he is," asserted Gregory.

"You're libelous, Captain Gregory," shouted the old gentleman.

"He was known all over town as the Irish dandy, Jack," answered the doctor. And they all roared, while Lord D'Arcy, to cover his confusion, had recourse to the decanter, from which he filled glasses for them all, and they drank merrily. Afterwards there was hot discussion and argument over Gregory's late orders; father and son bullying their old friend till he was stamping about the room in a rage. The conversation was interrupted by the entrance of a footman.

"What is it?" asks my lord.

"A note from the Marquis of G——, my lord," said the man.

"From whom?" cried both D'Arcys in the same breath, springing to their feet.

"From the Marquis of G——, my lord, and a reply is wanted."

Lord D'Arcy had broken the wax and was reading eagerly by this time, Jack and the doctor looking on in wonder.

"What is it, father?" questioned the young man.

"Take it. What do you make of it yourself?"

D'Arcy read aloud: "The Marquis of G—— presents his compliments to Lord and Major D'Arcy, and begs the pleasure of their company to supper on Thursday night."

"Is that all?" asked Gregory.

"Every word," said my lord.

"He's damned impertinent," said Jack.

"I quite agree with you, my son. Say no answer, James."

"Yes, my lord," and the footman was taking leave; but Gregory barred the way.

"Are you two in your right minds?" he cried. "You've both been berating me over a mere difference of opinion; but can there be any difference of opinion here? Who is it has been blocking your path at every step? Who is it has the power to remove every obstacle to your happiness, and send Jack back to his regiment? It's the Marquis of G——. This invitation is Heaven sent, and only God knows why. Would you cast it back in his face?"

"You speak sense—on occasion, Greg," said the old lord, wavering.

"I'll not go," said Jack, sullenly.

"You shall," said Gregory, "or I resign my commission this very day."

"He is right, Jack; we must pocket our pride," said the old man. "Wait, James." And sitting down, Lord D'Arcy wrote an acceptance to "the Marquis of G——'s courteous invitation," which Gregory approved, and it was sent off much against the advice of the hot-headed Major, who tried his best to thrust aside the great opportunity that Chance had poked under his nose.

CHAPTER V

The mysterious summons to sup with the Marquis of G—— caused much speculation in the house of D'Arcy, and yet before the Thursday arrived Gregory had convinced even Jack that it would have been absurd to refuse the invitation. He had been tremendously aided in this by dear little Lady D'Arcy, whose influence with her two hot-heads, as she called the old lord and Jack, was ridiculously out of proportion with the diminutive size of the lady herself. She had the permanent head of the family—which was fortunate, for Lord D'Arcy and his son were constantly losing theirs—and in all crises assumed directorship, though my lord stormed and the Major faintly rebelled. It was a united family, though, when Thursday night came and the little directress with a trembling heart gave them ''God speed'' as they drove off in the chariot.

53

The Marquis of G—— was a somewhat mysterious nobleman. The head of one of the most powerful Tory families in the kingdom, he had not been actively engaged in politics since his youth, and yet there was no more potent influence at Windsor or in Downing street than his. The secret of it was not known, but its existence was never questioned by members of either party, and even such active upholders of the opposition as Mr. Fox, Mr. Burke and Mr. Pitt acknowledged his power, while they recognized the futility of grappling with anything that seemed so impalpable. He was seldom seen about the town, confining his sociability to a small circle of intimates, and to the younger generation of Londoners his face was unknown. Years before, when White's was at its height, he and Lord D'Arcy— both young gallants of the town—had an unfortunate rencontre, over a matter that did little credit to either of them, and the Irishman had not come off second best. They had never met since, and it was with rather mixed feelings that the Lord D'Arcy alighted at his old-time antag-

onist's door, in Great Portland street.
They were much behind the hour—they
were bidden for eleven—and the latest of
the guests; for the street was already
filled with chariots, sedans, and hackney
coaches, while the loud talk of lounging
coachmen, footmen and chairmen showed
that their masters had been long inside.

As they entered the long, brilliant draw-
ing-room, the first of the evening's several
curious incidents—as D'Arcy, looking
back, remembered—took place. The
hum of talk subsided as the powdered,
pompous lackey announced: "My Lord
D'Arcy, Major D'Arcy," and, from the
brilliant group of men, one came quickly
toward them, who held his arm in a silken
sling. It was the young nephew of the
Marquis of G——; the same who had
crossed swords so unfortunately with
D'Arcy six months before. With a
slight trace of awkwardness and restraint,
he bade them welcome—the company
watching covertly—saying that his uncle
had been unexpectedly detained, and had
deputed him to receive the guests. Lord
D'Arcy was very gracious, and the Major

was so simple and jolly that what might have been a bad minute was passed over charmingly. No introductions were needed, and soon the old Irishman was in the midst of òld cronies exchanging snuff and gossip, while the young one was gaily chaffing with a group of friends and brother-officers.

In an alcove at the end, the card tables were set, and a group of inveterate gamblers were indulging in ombre and faro. Their reputations for reckless play had drawn a large group of on-lookers, and the Major found himself leaning over one of the tables, where the play was heaviest, an interested spectator. So interested that it was only suddenly he became conscious, that the buzz of voices in the rooms had ceased. He looked up quickly, and saw his father advancing beside a man nearly as tall as the old lord himself, and whose face had the fascination of familiarity. A step further toward him, and recognition brought the whole weird scene before his eyes: the inky night, the glimmer of the dim lamp, the shivering horses, and an old man with his back braced against the coach-panels, fighting for his life. "Blunt!" he cried, rushing toward them.

"Blunt?" said his father, stepping back in amazement, for he had heard the tale a dozen times.

"Major D'Arcy, allow me to present my uncle, the Marquis of G——," his nephew was saying.

"Good God!" ejaculated D'Arcy, "are you the Marquis of G——?"

"Good God, are you Blunt?" cried the old Irishman, looking from the Marquis to his son in a stupefied way that set the crowd shouting.

"I was traveling incog," said the old nobleman, grasping D'Arcy's hand. "This young gentleman wouldn't have given me a lift if he had known who I was," he added, his shrewd eyes twinkling, in anticipation of the youngster's embarrassment.

"I should have given you a lift, my lord," answered Jack quickly, with a laugh, "but I should have left you to the tender mercies of the gentleman we met on the road afterwards."

"You're a worthy son of old Jack," said the Marquis gaily, wringing the young man's hand again, and pleased at his boldness. "Come, you dullards," he cried, going up to the gamesters. "Do you think I asked you here to loot one another's purses?" And he unceremoniously swept cards and stakes off on to the floor. "To supper," he said, turning to the company; and leading the way with Lord D'Arcy on his right arm and Jack on his left, they entered the dining-room.

It was a brilliant throng that sat at table: the choice of London's fashion, wit, and powerful; and their host's entertainment was worthy of them and of him. The crackle of jests was incessant, and but served to whet the appetite for the good talk that followed. Gossip slipped up on one side of the table and down the other; the war in the colonies was discussed, and the vicious attitude of France; the ministry was criticised, and Mr. George Washington with his tatterdemalion forces was riddled with witty ridicule; the punch-bowl was emptied and

refilled and emptied again, and useless
bottles multiplied apace.

There were few, if any, of the guests
who knew of D'Arcy's and the Marquis of
G——'s adventure in the coach, and all,
who had seen the young soldier rush forward and greet his host as "Blunt," were
puzzled, though they all laughed at Jack's
unfeigned consternation and Lord D'Arcy's
astonishment. It was not till after, when
pipe-bowls were aglow, and the serious
work of digestion had begun, that any
explanation was forthcoming. The old
Marquis had risen from his seat at the
head of the table, and waiting a moment
for silence, raised his glass and said:
"Gentlemen, I give you His Majesty,
King George." Every man was on his
feet in an instant and drained the toast.
"And now," added my Lord Marquis, "I
have one other toast." He leaned forward on the table, and his piercing eyes
traveled down the long board till they
rested on his nephew standing at the
other end. "It needs some explanation,"
he said, "and though I fear to weary
you, it gives me the greatest pleasure to

give it. For some years my family, and
that of one of my guests to-night have
been on terms of very cordial enmity.
Within the year, the youngsters of both
houses have seen fit to add fuel to the fire
of the old feud, and it seemed likely to
mix us all in a very pretty quarrel." He
paused for a moment, and his cold little
smile hovered over the faces of his per-
plexed guests, who were wondering if the
old nobleman had gone daft. "Fortunately," he continued, "any such issue has
been averted. A few nights ago, I stood
in direst peril of my life, and in the very
last moment of respite, I was saved by the
courage and skill of the young gentleman,
who had been using both against my own
flesh and blood. I understand on the
very highest authority that this young
gentleman is leaving shortly to join his
regiment in the colonies, and I want to
thank him publicly in this manner before he is out of my reach. I give
you, gentlemen, Major John Gerald
D'Arcy."

There was a cry of "D'Arcy, D'Arcy,"
from all over the room, and the young

Irishman could have slipped through the floor. His head was reeling, and he could only grasp the hand of his new friend and murmur: "You are too good to me, my lord, you are too good to me."

"I can never repay the debt I owe you," said the old Marquis, simply, and his voice quavered. The next moment they were surrounded. The story of Dick Conyngham's luckless attack was told once more, and it was the excuse for a seeming bottomless punch-bowl. The night grew riotous, and it was not till the sun, streaming in through the curtain-guarded windows, put to shame the feeble yellow of the guttering candles that the company broke up.

The "Gazette," the next day, announced that "Major John Gerald D'Arcy, of the Grenadier Guards, having completely recovered from his severe wound received in the action at White Plains, New York, has been assigned to active duty on the staff of General, Lord Cornwallis." It was less than a fortnight after, that D'Arcy and Gregory set sail in the transport "Aurore," bound for the seat of war in the rebellious colonies. A mysterious Marquis can accomplish many things if he has a mind to.

CHAPTER VI

A CONTINENTAL DRAGOON

The same old whimsical Chance that meddles in the smaller affairs of men, twisting and untwisting the courses of their lives, is equally fond of mixing in their larger destinies. It had laid a heavy and ironic hand on the little colonial town of Philadelphia, in Pennsylvania, at the very beginning of the revolutionary struggle; whirling it into the storm center of the revolting colonies, hopelessly dividing its staid citizens against one another, and making its cognomen—the City of Brotherly Love—a mockery in the mouths of men.

The loyal subjects of good and wise King George—for the most part, thrifty Quakers and holders of lucrative office under the crown—looked on with dismay at the wild excesses of their fellow townsmen, culminating in the demagogic Declaration of Independence, and predicted the full and devastating wrath of the Gods. The mill of those revengeful Deities seemed to be grinding faster and finer than was its usual wont, in seeming verification of the prophecy, when that presumptuous mortal, George Washington, swooped down on the carousing Hessians at Trenton, and for the moment threw the machinery out of gear.

It took long winter and spring months to repair the damage; Lord Cornwallis, on the very point of taking passage for home, was hastily recalled, to chastise the unheard of audacity of the rebels, and in the course of events got rather the worst of it. The Philadelphia rabble and that traitorous assembly, the so-called Continental Congress, led on by such arch-traitors as John Adams, Thomas Jefferson, Morris, Randolph, and others of the same ilk, took heart once more, and while they grew more violent and seditious day by day, even dared to lay hands on the loyalists, who still gloried in their allegiance to King George.

But the summer was passing and retribution was at hand. Sir William Howe, with a picked army of seventeen or eighteen thousand men, had set out from New York to redeem the benighted town from the clutches of His Majesty's enemies. The loyalists were once more jubilant, and now it was the turn of the rebellious seceders to take their place on the anxious seat. None among them occupied it more restlessly than the little Towneshend household, whose fortunes for the next five months are inextricably bound up in this Tale.

The Towneshend family held high place in old Colonial Philadelphia. The head of the house, Benjamin Towneshend, the youngest son of a youngest son, forced into expatriation by the resistless English law of primogeniture, had settled on the hospitable banks of the Schuylkill and drifted into the channels of trade. Industry, acuteness and the West Indies had brought him a liberal fortune, while breeding and good looks fetched a charming wife, and later came two wonderful children. Success smiled upon him before the young blood in man and wife had run its course, and while they still could enjoy its bounty. The marvelous stone house, the wonder of the country-side at the time, was built, and the ornate gardens, after the dear old English style, were laid out with hedges of box and clipped yew. It became one of the very few centers of gaiety in the prim little commonwealth.

The daughter was one of the beauties of the town, and no lovelier penitent stepped from chariot every Sunday and marched up the aisle of Christ Church, nor gayer, sprightlier maid danced minuet at the assemblies, than Pamela Towneshend. She was a great housewife too, and something of a hoyden besides, if neighbors' reports were to be believed, for she rode as dashingly as her brother Edward, and was his companion and equal on many a shooting and fishing trip about the country. All of which filled her father's heart with pride, and turned the heads of half the youngsters in the colony.

Then came the journey to London, where the youngest of the youngest met the eldest of the eldest, a man of fashion and title, who was very glad to know his wealthy colonial relative and his "Indian

children," as he jokingly called Pamela
and her brother.

A gay season followed, during which the
fluttering mamma feared and trembled for
her daughter, who became one of the belles
at Tunbridge, and even had the supreme
honor of a compliment and toast from
the incomparable Beau Beamish himself.

But the gladness of it all was terribly
eclipsed by the sudden illness and death of
the father, and it was then that Pamela
showed first what burdens her young
shoulders were capable of bearing. Edward
was but a lad of nineteen, she four
years his senior, and her mother, wilting
like a stricken flower, looked to her for
help and guidance. It was a sad home-
going, and the big house seemed blighted
by the family's trouble. Pamela was
equal to it all, however; she changed
places with her mother, who faded into a
heartbroken invalid, and took up the
household reins with a firm hand. With
the invaluable help of their neighbor and
her father's old friend, the Quaker, Sam-
uel Davis, the many business interests
were straightened out; and her cousin,

Cynthia Deane, coming to live with them, brought a ray of sunshine into the big house, and something more to young Edward.

Two years slipped by, and the cloud of grief was only just lifting, when signs of the coming political storm grew ominous; and a year later the storm broke in all its fury, carrying Edward, his sister's joy and his cousin Cynthia's sweetheart, off in the maelstrom. He was a lieutenant in the City Troop, an eager, gallant, patriotic lad, and in spite of the protests of their Tory neighbor, Davis, his mother and the girls bade him go with an heroic joyfulness. And he journeyed to the camp of His Excellency, General George Washington, with a present of a thousand · golden guineas for the cause. His gallantry at the disastrous battle of Long Island brought him promotion, and later, after that terrible Christmas night, crossing the Delaware, he was honored by a position on the staff of the Commander-in-Chief.

His fervent letters to the little household kept their spirits high, and their hearts firm; much needed stimulants were they,

as the days grew dark and calamity threat-
ened. It was late in August, '77, that the
rebel army marched through Philadelphia
on its way to meet the British, then
dropping anchor in Delaware Bay. The
devoted women had a hurried glimpse of
their boy, who snatched an hour to be
with them, and then he was gone again,
while for them was the harder task of
waiting, waiting, waiting. On the 12th of
September came the news of Washington's
defeat the day before, at the Brandywine.
The town was in an uproar; Congress
bundled up its records and fled to Lan-
caster; the streets were full of timid pa-
triots flying they knew not where, and the
loyal Tories were exultant, openly at last.

No word came from the young aid-
de-camp at the front; and as the days
passed, sickening dread took full possession
of the house; Pamela alone bearing up
and refusing to give in to the horrible fore-
boding. A fortnight passed. It was
early one morning when Cynthia came from
the house to take her daily last look at the
already autumn-stricken flowers. There
were a gallant, sturdy few, that still

colored the beds, and to these she was
bending, when she heard a quick step on
the path behind her. She turned, and
her heart leaped. "Ned!" she cried.
"Safe—safe——" she would have fallen,
but he had her in his arms; his lips were
on her cheek. "Cynthia," she heard him
whisper, and she thrilled in consciousness
again, as he repeated it.

"Did I frighten you, dear?" he asked,
smiling.

"Oh, Ned, we had given up hope."

"And Pamela and mother, they are
well?"

"Yes, and they'll be overjoyed to welcome you from——" she faltered, and he
clasped her to him.

"From what, sweetheart?"

"The dead," she answered, drooping at
the memory of the anxious days.

"Then you've missed me?" he asked
tenderly, with a lover's unkindness.

"Missed you?" she faltered, and her
eyes swam as she drew his face to her and
kissed him. "How I've missed you!
And the army?" she asked timidly. "All
is lost? You have surrendered?"

"Surrendered!" he cried. "Never. They've driven us back, inch by inch, but they've paid dearly for their passage."

"The way is clear for them, then?"

"The British will enter Philadelphia this morning," he answered. "It is the happiest chance that I am here to warn you. The General hurried me back with important dispatches for Mr. Reid, one of our agents here. I've been in the saddle since five this morning."

"Poor boy, you are worn out."

"It is nothing," he answered, "if I can but get you to a place of safety."

. "Don't fear for us, dear. Pamela will take care of us."

"Oh, I know she has the courage of a lion," he said, "but she's a woman, after all."

"And Mr. Davis will be near at hand," suggested Cynthia.

"A pretty protector!" laughed the young soldier. "A Tory Quaker, forever preaching non-resistance."

"He has been very kind to us."

"Oh, yes," answered Towncshend, a look of impatience crossing his face, "I know he would be that. But his kindliness will hardly impress the sensibilities of a Hessian Yager, or a British Grenadier."

"You must not be afraid for us, Ned," she cried, bravely. "What harm could come to us here?"

"I can't help but fear for you, can I? All that's dearest to me in the world, mother, sister, sweetheart, shut up in Philadelphia, and in the hands of the enemy. Oh, if Pamela had only listened to reason when I was here last month, and let me have moved you out of harm's way!"

"You know, dear, that Aunt Clarissa could not have stood any journey," ventured Cynthia, trying to quiet the boy's fears.

"I know, I know," he answered. "Mother is too delicate for any change, which frightens me all the more for her safety here."

"Oh, my boy, you are tired and worried. Come into the house and see your mother and Pamela. It will rest you." She took his arm gently, and they turned toward the house, the dusty, travel-

stained, wearied young officer leaning on
her in his perplexity. They were mounting the steps to the little terrace, when
Pamela and her mother issued from the
door. Their cheeks blanched at the sight
of him, but he was kissing their color back
again before they could cry out.

"It's Ned, mother, it's Ned!" cried
Pamela, her face aglow.

But the mother knew too well; she held
him in her frail arms and wept as she
murmured brokenly, "My boy, my boy."

They all turned to the garden again,
and there under the old trees he told
them the disastrous story.

"And the British?" questioned Pamela,
her eyes flashing.

"They will occupy the town to-day;
they may be here at any moment."

"And you?" she asked.

"You must thank their tardiness for
this sight of me. I couldn't have stopped
had they been here."

"Where do you go from here?" asked
Cynthia.

"To headquarters at Chester. I don't
know the General's plans, but I think

once Sir William Howe and Lord Cornwallis are arrived in Philadelphia, they'll
find some trouble leaving it. Dear
mother," he added, turning to her, "I am
so anxious for you all."

"Never fear, my boy," she answered,
bravely, "the British would never molest
such a harmless old lady; and Pamela and
Cynthia will take good care of me."

"That we will, dear aunt," said Cynthia.

"If, as I think, the General's plan is to
sit down and watch," went on the young
man, "I'll not be far away, and will see
you often——"

"You must not risk it, Ned," put in
his sister.

"No one knows the country hereabouts
as I do, Pamela," he answered, "and a
hundred different paths will bring me,
that the enemy knows nothing of."

"There are dangers enough on every
hand without my boy seeking new ones,"
said his mother, gently.

"Never fear, dear mother. And
Pamela, neither you nor Cynthia must
venture out alone."

"Foolish boy!" she answered, "we'll

74

take care of ourselves. The British are not ogres. They'll not eat us."

"They had better not try," laughed Cynthia, taking his hand. "You should see Pamela, Ned, with the new pistols you gave her before you went away. Every night, when Sambo is locking up, she stalks beside him, a pistol in either hand, as fierce as any grenadier."

"Hush, you silly child," laughed Pamela.

"I warrant you she'd use 'em too, on occasion," rejoined Towneshend.

"She shares with my boy, her father's courage," said the fond mother.

"She will join the army yet, if we don't watch her, aunt," went on the teasing Cynthia.

"Oh, if I were a man——" Pamela was beginning when Cynthia again broke in:

"Why let a little matter of sex deter you? You shoot and ride as well as Ned now, and I've no doubt you'd soon handle his saber better."

The banter would have gone on interminably, for their spirits fairly bubbled over at the joy of the reunion, but interruption came in the shape of a tall figure that advanced toward them from the house. He was upon them almost before they were aware.

"It's Mr. Davis," said Cynthia, who first espied him.

"So it is," said Towneshend, as the straight old Quaker came up.

He was a giant in size, and he leaned on a huge walking-stick as he gave them greeting. "Good morning, friends," he said, his kindly gray eye taking in the little group at a glance, "this is a family party I scarce expected to find."

"Our boy has surprised us all this morning, friend Davis," said the happy mother.

"What is thee doing here, Edward?" asked the old man, smiling grimly. "Does thee bring Mr. Washington's terms of surrender?"

"No," answered Towneshend, good humoredly, "but *General* Washington is at any time willing to submit terms of surrender to Sir William Howe."

"Is that so, Edward? Does thee know it to be so?" said Davis, eagerly.

"I would stake my life on it," answered the young officer.

"What is this, Ned?" questioned Pamela, almost harshly, not noticing the twinkle in her brother's eye.

"This is great news thee brings," went on the Quaker, "and what are the terms?"

"I think the General would grant Sir William the same terms he gave General Rall at Trenton," said Towneshend.

"What does thee mean?" asked Davis sharply, his face coloring.

"I mean that nothing but the complete capitulation of Sir William and his army would satisfy the Commander-in-Chief," declared the young man, while Pamela and Cynthia both clapped their hands.

"Art thou mad, boy?" said the old man, knitting his ragged brows.

"On the contrary," answered Towneshend, "it is only a question of time. You had better come over to us before it's too late," he added.

"Never!" said Davis, and his firm old mouth drew tense and hard.

"Well, dear old friend," said the boy, seeing that he had gone a little beyond the jesting bounds, "we won't quarrel at this late day over a difference of opinion."

"You'll live to accept mine," rejoined the Quaker.

"I trust not," answered Towneshend, gravely. "But you have been too good to me and mine for me ever to forget it."

"Oh, rubbish!" ejaculated the old man, uncomfortably.

"And now, dear ones," said the young man, glancing at his watch, "I must get to horse. I've a long journey before me. I know you'll watch over them for me, Mr. Davis."

"I promise thee, lad, I promise thee," said the other, grasping his hand.

They made the parting a gay one, while their voices gave the lie to the words of glad good-bye. And then he was gone, his tall young figure disappearing through the gateway, and the clatter of his horse's hoofs striking at the hearts of the dear ones he left.

CHAPTER VII

A FRIEND INDEED

The little group sat silent, till Davis, thinking to relieve the tension, and in some small way detract attention from his own emotion, ejaculated:

"Drat the boy! I could stand it, if he were fighting on the other side."

His diversion was a success, for Pamela turned on him. "He is fighting for the right."

"Woman's rubbish," said the old Quaker, testily. "I am glad his father can't see him in that uniform."

"His father would have been as proud of him as I am, friend Davis," answered Mrs. Towneshend, with a gentle dignity.

"No good can come of rebellion against our rulers," said the old man.

"We are no longer rebels, Mr. Davis," interrupted Cynthia, "we have claimed freedom for our own."

"Aye, claimed it," said Davis, taking a pinch of snuff and smiling at her. He had succeeded more wisely than he had planned. His three gentle friends were up in arms at his Toryism, and for a moment the pain at parting from their boy was stopped. Mrs. Towneshend had risen and started slowly toward the house, the others following. At the steps, Pamela turned to him with her frank smile, and put out her hand; and he knew he was forgiven. The stiff, unbending old man liked these reconciliations with the girl whom he loved as a daughter.

"You must take lunch with us, Mr. Davis," she said.

"Not for the world, my dear. I have a thousand businesses to attend. There is no offense at my words, Mrs. Towneshend?" he asked of the old lady, who stood on the steps above.

"None," she smiled sweetly, "old friends have privilege of free speech."

"Thee knows I love the boy," said the old Quaker, heartily.

"I do," she said, and turned once more to the house.

"I want to speak with thee and Cynthia a moment," whispered Davis to Pamela, as she moved off.

"I'll be in in a moment, mother dear," called Pamela, as her mother entered the house. "What is it?" she asked, turning to him. "Can Cynthia or I do anything for you?"

"Not for me, Pamela, but for thyselves."

"What is it?" questioned Cynthia, while her cousin looked at him with a vague fear in her eyes.

"I greatly fear that the British will take possession of thy house," said the old man, deliberately.

"Take possession of our house!" cried Pamela. "What do you mean?"

"They will probably use it for quartering some new officers," said Davis. "I didn't wish to alarm thy mother; but the house is so conveniently situated that it will hardly escape requisition."

"What shall we do, Pamela?" questioned Cynthia, timidly.

"We shall not move one inch," answered her cousin, and her lithe, strong figure

81

seemed to harden, as if in opposition to an attacking British regiment.

"I hardly see any alternative, my dear," said the old man, kindly. "My house is at thy disposal though, for as a loyalist, I shall not be interfered with."

"I thank you, Mr. Davis, for your kindness," said the girl, "but we shall stay here till we are driven out. And surely, Sir William Howe and My Lord Cornwallis would not stoop to that?"

"They will not drive thee out, but doubtless some officers will be quartered here," rejoined Davis.

"So be it," answered Pamela, "there is ample room for a whole company of officers, and us besides."

"Do listen to Mr. Davis, Pamela," interrupted Cynthia, timidly. "We are quite alone and helpless."

"We will stay," rejoined Pamela, firmly, and then, with a smile: "But why worry about a thing till it happens? The desirability of our lodgings may be entirely overlooked."

"Well, I'm content if Pamela is," said Cynthia, resignedly.

"Thou art a self-willed young hussy," said the Quaker, taking snuff violently.

"Please don't call me names," said Pamela, going to him contritely, "we are quite safe here, and mother is really not well enough to stand any change."

"Don't mind my growling, Pamela," he answered. "I am only concerned for thy welfare. Thou art a brave lass."

Their talk had been so animated and of such interest to them all, that it was little wonder no one of them had heard the click of the gate, at the far end of the gardens; nor were they aware of the approach of the two soldiers, till the clank of sabers and spurs wheeled all three around in surprise. The intruders were foreigners; their fierce, black, upturned mustachios and gaudy uniforms proclaimed them Hessians at a glance. They came on with an offensive swagger, the moment they saw they were under notice. As they drew near, the evident senior addressed himself to Davis in harsh, broken English, that was barely intelligible to the listeners.

"Are you the rebel owner of this house?" he asked.

"I am neither the owner of this house, nor am I a rebel," answered the old man, quietly.

"You can't escape us, old shoebuckles, by denying your colors," said the other, coarsely.

"That he can't," said the first. "And do these pretty maids belong with the house?" His eyes ran the girls over, as if he were appraising sheep. They drew closer together, but their stare was so haughty and direct that he dropped his eyes and laughed uneasily.

"Coy, are you? We'll change all that before long, eh, Millhausen?" he · said, turning to his companion.

"That will we, Captain," answered the other. "The spoils of war, eh?"

Their vulgarity was so brutal, and the surprise of their appearance so sudden, that the little group was dazed.

"Come, old man, we shall want all your keys. I trust your cellars are in good condition," said the Captain, and then turning to Millhausen, "There'll be room for four of us here."

"I am in charge of this house," said Pamela, stepping a trifle forward.

"You, pretty one?" ejaculated the Captain. "So much the better."

She paid no notice to his insolence, but there was that in her eyes that spoke to them more plainly than stinging words.

"By what authority do you force yourself on our hospitality?" she asked.

"You use big words, my maid," said one.

"By the authority of our strong right arms. You are ours," said the other, brutally.

"I shall report your insolence to Sir William Howe, and he will have you publicly whipped."

"Ha, my little wildcat," cried Millhausen, "I see we shall have to tame you."

"That we shall," laughed the Captain.

He made a step toward her, and Pamela involuntarily shrank back, the utter loathing she felt for the creatures, showing in physical retreat. Davis, who had stood calmly looking on during this colloquy, stepped in front of the girls, his massive figure almost screening them from view.

"Out of the way, you old fool," cried the Hessian, exasperated by the imperturbability of the placid Friend.

"I said I was not the owner of this house," said Davis, "but I am in a certain way the guardian of its inmates. Pamela," he said, "thee had better go into the house with Cynthia. I will talk with these gentlemen."

"Stand aside," yelled Millhausen, his face inflamed with anger. He rushed at Davis, thinking to sweep by him, through mere force, but it was like charging a stone wall. The old man threw him back, and nearly off his feet. The girls seemed paralyzed with fear, and stood motionless. The other officer had stepped quickly behind them, and placed himself in front of the door.

"Thee had better let the young women pass," said Davis, turning to him.

"I'll spit you like a chicken," cried the infuriated man, whom he had thrown off.

"For heaven's sake, Mr. Davis, give way," cried Pamela, fearfully.

"If thee doesn't put up thy sword, I'll take it from thee," replied the Quaker. The red was mounting to his cheeks, and his fingers gripped the heavy stick he carried, as in a vice.

"Curse his insolence; run the rebel through!" yelled the one at the door. No such encouragement was needed. With an oath on his lips, he drew his saber and sprang at the old man. The big cane swung dexterously through the air, there was a smash on the villain's sword-arm, and his blade flew in the air.

"Damn you!" he screamed in an agony, clasping his arm that hung limp; and then he yelled to his companion: "Kill him, Raab!"

"Thee had better hold thy distance," said Davis, keeping them well in his front.

"I'll teach you!" roared the man, and was rushing for him venomously, when a loud "halloa" from the garden gate arrested him. All turned, and hurrying toward them were two in the gayest scarlet. The younger man as they approached doffed his hat with a gallant air, and tak-

ing in the situation with laughing eyes,
addressed himself to Pamela:

"I trust you will pardon this intrusion,
ladies. Captain Gregory and I have evidently interrupted your friends' morning
broadsword exercise."

The brogue was none but D'Arcy's.

"You have interrupted two villains in
an infamous attack on an unarmed old
man and two defenseless girls," cried
Pamela, stepping forward, her cheeks and
eyes ablaze, her breast heaving with heavy
anger.

"And is it so, my dear young lady?"
asked D'Arcy, gently; he turned and ran
a cold, insolent eye up and down the
Hessian officers, and then, with a con-
tempt that even they could feel, he remarked: "Faith, handsome does as
handsome is; and they're not much on
looks, are they, Greg?" He appealed to
his friend, who was fidgeting about, knowing only too well what that mocking voice
meant.

"For heaven's sake, Jack," he whispered, "don't pick a quarrel."

"Hist, man," answered D'Arcy, aloud,

"they don't want to fight, they only want to bully old men and ladies."

"Who the devil are you?" said Millhausen, furiously.

"Major D'Arcy, Grenadier Guards," answered the Irishman, "and I'll thank you for just a trifle more of civility," he added, coldly.

"You be——" the German was putting in gruffly, when D'Arcy interrupted:

"Tut—tut, man. Before ladies!" He turned to them courteously; his deference was beautiful to behold. "May I beg of you to withdraw? These——" he hesitated, that his words might reach the proper ears—"these officers are evidently not accustomed to the presence of your sex."

"It is a pity that His Majesty is forced to require such unpresentable allies," said Pamela, cuttingly.

"Madam," answered the young officer, bowing very low, "I heartily agree with you."

The girls swept him a courtesy, and disappeared into the house.

"Damn your impudence!" said the

senior of the Hessians. "You shall answer to us for this."

Davis, who ever since the Grenadier's appearance had watched his gallant figure, and listened in amazement and with a sort of fascination to his remarks, now stepped forward. "I beg of you, gentlemen, that this shall go no further."

"I don't know your name, old Mr. Drab-clothes," said D'Arcy, with an amused smile, "but you've had your fun, and I won't be done out of mine. I never permit insolence from mustachios," he added, turning to the Germans.

"For God's sake, Jack, what will the General say?" interrupted Gregory, in a frenzy at the young Irishman's indiscretion.

"My seconds will call upon you to-day," cried the Captain.

"And mine," said Millhausen. "Where are you quartered?"

"My friend Captain Gregory will make all arrangements for me. We shall be quartered here. Good morning." And turning on his heel, he engaged in conversation with Gregory and Davis, while the Hessians stamped furiously out of the gardens.

CHAPTER VIII

UNWELCOME GUESTS

"A pretty mess," growled Gregory, as they disappeared.

"I pray thee, sir, to reconsider this," said old Davis.

"Tut, sir," answered D'Arcy. "I won't hurt 'em; only teach 'em good manners."

"Did I understand thee to say that thee and thy friend would be quartered here?" asked the Quaker, anxiety for the girls getting the better of his desire to stop a duel.

"Yes," replied the Irishman, "and very fair quarters they are, too," he added, looking up at the house.

"I trust we will not incommode the ladies," said Gregory.

"It is that, that I would speak about," answered the old man. "Mrs. Towneshend and her daughter and niece are quite alone here. Mrs. Towneshend is an invalid, and the occupation of her house, I fear, would distress her exceedingly.'

"You don't think we would hurt the women?" replied Gregory. "*We're* not Hessians."

"My house, sirs, not a quarter of a mile away, is quite at your disposal," said Davis.

"It is already occupied, my good sir," D'Arcy answered.

"Occupied!" cried the Quaker, in dismay. "But I am a loyalist."

"Then you'll be overjoyed to hear that Lord Cornwallis has his headquarters there," laughed Gregory.

"My dear sir," said D'Arcy, kindly, feeling for the old man's discomfiture, "I like the way you handled those rascally Dutchmen. Your friends will be much safer with us in the house, than on the outside. We will serve to keep such vermin out, and shall be very little trouble. Two bedrooms and a living room are all we require."

"I thank thee, sir, for thy consideration," answered Davis. "I will go in and tell them."

"A militant Quaker," Gregory remarked a moment later, as the tall gray figure entered the house.

"Don't talk to me of Quakers," cried Jack. "It's she, I'm thinking of. Greg, me boy, she's a duchess in disguise."

"Who is a duchess in disguise?" asked the doctor, blankly.

"Oh, ye lump of ice! You're as lukewarm as weak tea!" rejoined the Irishman. "Didn't you notice the dark girl with the grand manner and the foot like a fairy?"

"And the tongue like a rapier?" questioned Gregory, laughing.

"Sure, you're an ungallant lout, Greg, like the rest of your countrymen. My lady has the gift of language and uses it," said D'Arcy.

"She must be Irish," answered Gregory.

"Faith, I can account for her in no other way," the young officer replied quickly.

"Oh, well," the doctor said, "no philandering, Jack."

"You're vulgar, Captain Gregory."

"I wish to the devil you had not quarreled with those fellows," the other put in, worried at the prospect.

"Don't bother, Greg. They're as clumsy as Englishmen, and I won't hurt 'em."

"If it comes to Lord Cornwallis' ears you'll be broke. He's expressly forbidden dueling."

"But you must see that no word of it gets out, me boy. That is, if you don't want to see me gazetted home again," said D'Arcy, gaily.

"You don't seem to realize that being on the staff, demands discretion," said Gregory, angrily.

"There's no such word in Irish," D'Arcy laughed.

"Lord D'Arcy would never see you, if you disgraced yourself again."

"He wouldn't recognize me as a son of his, if I didn't," answered the young officer in huge spirits.

"Well, I refuse to act as your second," rejoined Gregory, now thoroughly out of humor.

The young grenadier always knew when

he had pressed the touchy old doctor beyond the limit, and immediately began to wheedle, throwing an arm affectionately about his shoulders.

"Now, Greg, dear, you're behaving unhandsomely. I've had only three fights since we landed," he coaxed.

"And each time you swore to me would be the last," answered Gregory, unrelenting.

"And I kept my oath," asserted D'Arcy.

"You kept your oath!" ejaculated the doctor, in disgust.

"Each time was the *last time*," pleaded his friend, disingenuously. "Come, Greg," he went on, "just this once. You wouldn't have the Dutch beggars laughing at the Guards?"

Gregory wavered. "You'll not hurt 'em?" he asked.

"'Pon me honor, Greg, I'll only disarm 'em."

"Jack D'Arcy, you'll ruin me along with yourself," said the old man, testily, annoyed at himself. "You wouldn't have bothered your head about the rascals, if it hadn't been for the little rebel wench inside."

"Greg, she's a lady, rebel or no rebel, and no gentleman could stand by and see her insulted."

"You'll have your hands full, if you're going to protect every little Colonial who has a neat ankle and a kissing mouth," said Gregory, drily.

"I'll take it unkindly, Greg, if you make any more disparaging remarks about the Duchess."

"Have it your own way," and the old doctor laughed.

"You'll second me?" asked D'Arcy, sure of his answer.

"I will. Have I ever refused?"

"No. You're a jewel," said the young Irishman. "And now scatter yourself and look after our baggage. I'll go in and arrange matters with our hostess."

Gregory was departing on his mission when D'Arcy called after, "Hurry back. I'm in the hands of the enemy." At that moment Pamela appeared in the doorway. The young man heard the opening door, and turned to her with his hat in his hand as she came toward him.

"We have to thank you, Major D'Arcy, for your very timely interference in our behalf," she said. There was no sign in her face that she had overheard his call to Gregory, and the young officer thought he had never seen so lovely a thing in his life as the tall girl, standing on the steps, looking down on him coldly, and with a certain condescension that seemed to him fitting.

"*I* should speak of gratitude, Miss Towneshend, in being permitted in any way to serve you," he said, gravely.

"Mr. Davis tells me that you and your companion have chosen our house for your lodging," went on Pamela, ignoring his last remark.

"The fortunes of war, Miss Towne·shend, throw us upon your bounty." He was determined to place the matter in its best light, but it was difficult to make way against the self-possession and imperturbability of the girl.

"The fortunes of war make us unwilling hosts," she said.

" 'Tis only the order of my chief, Lord Cornwallis, that forces your hospitality. He has directed Captain Gregory and myself to lodge here," answered D'Arcy, feeling the absolute necessity of meeting the hostile criticism that shone from those gray eyes.

"I do not wish to seem ungracious nor unmindful of your chivalrous defense of my cousin and myself," said the girl, feeling his sincerity, "but I cannot forget that you are an enemy to my country. Whatever you and Captain Gregory need shall be freely given, but—" she wavered for a moment, and he could see her eyes fill, "but I hate your being here," she added, vehemently.

D'Arcy was touched, her tears brought a feeling of debasement, of unmanliness, that he should be the cause of her torment.

"Dear young lady," he said, quickly, "you make me feel no better than one of those rascally Hessians."

His eagerness brought a smile to her lips. "Oh, you are better than they," she said.

"I thank you for the slightest commendation, Miss Towneshend, though it
come from the most odious comparison,"
answered D'Arcy.

"We judge a man by his friends; a soldier by his allies," said Pamela.

"I never thought of that," he replied,
"and you're quite right."

"We should be thankful that *they* are
not to be our guests," said she.

"I shall twist that into a half welcome,
at least."

"God forbid, that British uniforms
should have even a half-welcome in our
house," Pamela answered, earnestly.

"I was never before tempted to desert
my colors," said D'Arcy, gallantly; but
pretty speeches, he felt, were unheeded
by that straightforward, dominating
creature, who so turned the tables,
that she made him feel like the vul-
garest intruder, instead of a conquering
hero.

They were interrupted by the reappear-
ance of Gregory, whom D'Arcy presented
immediately.

"I will show you the house, gentlemen," she said, simply, "and you may choose your chambers."

"We follow, Miss Towneshend," answered D'Arcy.

She passed on ahead through the doorway. At the top of the steps, D'Arcy stopped his companion and ejaculated, "Greg, me boy, I was mistaken, she's not a duchess in disguise."

"What!" laughed Gregory, "so soon disillusioned? Is she more like a chamber wench?"

"Hush, man, you blaspheme," answered the young officer. "She's every inch a queen!"

CHAPTER IX

The rebel capital bent its head meekly, not to say graciously, to the yoke of the conquerors. There was a brief moment of suspense and hope, when Washington came battering at the gates, one October morning, but the cartloads of wounded trundled through the streets, from Germantown, later in the day, showed that his plans had gone awry, and the little town settled down with no very ill grace, it must be said, to enjoy its captivity.

The weeks passed, drifting slowly into months, and the Doctor and D'Arcy, who, with many another besides, fretted at the enforced idleness, found some compensation in the comfort of their lodgings. The little affair with the Hessian officers went off very comically, and was the occasion of many a witty sally at the expense of D'Arcy—always behind his back, it must be said. They had met early one

103

morning in a secluded corner of the town,
and the two bullies had been taught a
lesson in swordsmanship, that was like to
last them the rest of their careers. The
Guards' mess laughed heartily over the
matter, and one night at a regimental
supper, at "The Indian Queen," young
Captain Dacier ventured to chaff the
Major about "the beauteous Miss Towneshend." He was saved by his friends,
however, who drew him off quickly, at the
sight of D'Arcy's peculiar little smile,
which most of them knew so well meant
trouble.

As for "the beauteous Miss Towneshend" herself, she tried valiantly to make
the best of circumstances that filled her
with chagrin. She bitterly resented the fes-
tive and gala air about the town; she would
have drunk the health of King George
as quickly as she would have attended
one of the gay, brilliant assemblies at the
"City Tavern," or made one of the jolly,
thoughtless little audiences at the theater
in South street. She would have consid-
ered herself false to every patriotic ideal, if
in any way she had condoned the presence

of the invaders, for whom she had a bitter, rankling hatred.

It concentrated on the two representatives whose red-coats flitted in and out of her house; and though their meetings were of the rarest, yet it was impossible not, at times, to come in contact with them; particularly as the only outlet from their apartments was through her favorite part of the house: the book room. There, on occasion, when her calculation as to their absence or time of return went amiss, they surprised her, and it became a matter of constant and eager speculation on D'Arcy's part, how often, during a week, he might hope to catch a glimpse of the tall, dark girl, whose very indifference was beginning to mean more to him than the smiles of any other woman ever had.

The preciousness of these chance meetings, though they profited him nothing more than a cold curtsy, or at best, the briefest of desultory talk, was tremendously augmented in the eyes of the young Irishman, by the fact that they were possible nowhere else. He had commenced going to the public assemblies and the private routs, with an eagerness of anticipation that he was sadly conscious of, only when he found that she never appeared. And the result was, that he became less and less a participator in the gaieties of his fellow officers; spending what time he had from his duties riding about the country by day, and at night, for the most time, playing sedately at piquet, with some older officer; while he developed a crotchety moodiness that was near driving Gregory frantic.

The old man watched over him solicitously, and during his absences puffed solemnly at his pipe for hours, in anxious cogitation as to the youngster's malady. Though he said little, his keen watchfulness worried D'Arcy almost to frenzy. He didn't want to be bothered; he wanted to nurse the deadly, hopeless feeling within him, by himself. He knew Gregory would never suspect the real trouble, and he dreaded the time when he should have to tell him; for he knew his old friend's loving inquisitiveness would force it from him sooner or later.

It came rather sooner than he expected.

It was one night, late. Gregory had a habit of slipping downstairs, in his dressing-gown, and smoking before the huge fire, till D'Arcy came in. He had asked and obtained permission from Pamela for his indulgence—neither of the men presumed an iota on their peculiar position in the house, and strove by every means in their power to establish the high standard of host and guest—and it was one of the pleasantest hours of the day to the old man, when the little household was long abed, and he sat smoking, with the decanter not too far away from his reach, and his slippered feet toasting on the fender. He was well through his fourth pipe this special night, before Jack put in an appearance, and it was an unsatisfactory one to his old friend. Discontent sat heavily on his face, and throwing off his cloak, he flung himself moodily into a chair.

"What is it, Jack?" asked Gregory.

"Oh, nothing's the matter; don't bother a fellow."

"Jack, I believe you're not well."

"Oh, you want to physic me," answered

D'Arcy. "Well, I'm not well," he went on.

"What is it?" asked Gregory, eagerly, sitting up.

"I have some trouble here," answered Jack, and he put his hand over his heart.

"Your heart?" ejaculated the doctor, his professional interest aroused, and blinding him to the gay twinkle that had come into D'Arcy's eyes.

"Where it ought to be," the Major replied.

"Nonsense," said Gregory. "You're as sound as a horse."

"Well, I ought to know," said D'Arcy.

"Tell me about it. What are your symptoms?" asked the old man, leaning forward, his brows screwed together critically.

"Greg, my appetite seems to be disappearing, and I'm losing interest in everything."

"I've noticed it," nodded the doctor, gravely.

"And whenever I see or think of a certain person," went on D'Arcy, "I have a tremendous palpitation in my heart."

"Jack D'Arcy, are you going mad?" cried Gregory, sitting up very straight, and staring.

"Maybe it's the same thing, Greg. I'm in love." It came out very gently, with a low laugh, and he felt as if he had dropped a burden the moment his secret had slipped through his lips.

"Well, I'll be damned!" ejaculated Gregory, and then he burst forth angrily. "Do you mean to say that you've worked me up to operation pitch with nothing but a tale of lovesickness?"

"You seem to think it's nothing serious," rejoined D'Arcy, hiding his merriment by a violent assault on the smoldering logs.

"What if it is serious?" said Gregory. "You don't suppose I keep love draughts on tap, do you?"

"You're unkind to me, Greg," said the Irishman, "you have no sentiment."

Gregory puffed contemptuously for a moment. "Who is it—this time?" he asked.

"I resent your 'this time,' Captain Gregory," answered D'Arcy, with pre-

tense of the offended. "You know bet-
ter than any one," he added, "that
I wasn't serious the last time with
Lady Gray, or the time before that with
Mrs. Germaine, or even with Lady Betty
Kew."

"Oh, Jack, you'll be the death of me,"
roared Gregory.

"Faith, I should like to be," said Jack.
"You've no more sympathy for the tender
passion than a stone."

"My sympathies are broad, Jack," said
the doctor, still laughing till the tears
ran, "but I've never been able to cover
your tender passions."

"You're mightily amused at my expense," said D'Arcy, a bit ruffled at the
other's continued amusement.

"Who is it, Jack?" gasped the old
man, between gurgles.

"I'll not call upon you to stretch your
elastic sympathy any further, Captain
Gregory," replied D'Arcy.

"Now, Jack, you know I was but teasing," coaxed Gregory.

"You'll not breathe it to a soul?"

"I swear not."

"It's the Duchess," whispered D'Arcy, as if the room held a company full.

"The Duchess?" questioned Gregory, mystified.

"Pamela," said D'Arcy.

"Pamela? You don't mean Miss Towneshend?" cried the doctor, and the mystery of weeks was flooded with light.

"Yes," answered the young Irishman, "the loveliest creature that ever tripped minuet, or killed with the glance of gray eyes. She was born under the ægis of divine Diana, and all the goddess' gifts have been showered on her," rhapsodized D'Arcy; then breaking off and jumping to his feet he exclaimed: "Oh, Greg, why haven't you heart enough to know what I'm talking about?"

"Too much heart addles the brains," said the old man, sententiously.

"Pah! Your blood runs icy cold," rejoined the Major. "Come up to bed, it's past one," he said, taking up his candle and leading the way. Gregory followed after, rather dazed at an earnestness in his young friend's man-

ner, that was unaccustomed, but re-
lieved withal that there was no physical
or mental derangement in his pro-
tégé.

CHAPTER X

A freezing December was drawing towards its end, and there was bitter vaticination in the shrewd and piercing air, for the devoted little American army scattered on the hills about Valley Forge. Young Captain Towneshend had managed once to get through the lines, shortly after the battle of Germantown, and at long intervals — they seemed eternities to Cynthia—hastily scribbled communications arrived at the Towneshend house, and were devoured by the three anxious women. The strain told perceptibly on the old lady, and Pamela was heartsick at her mother's worried, pitiable condition. She appealed hurriedly to Gregory one night, when her mother appeared to be in a dangerous state, and the old doctor worked wonders, and continued to watch over her till she was quite on the mend. He managed to break through the barrier

113

of distrust, too, that the girls defended so
zealously against every approach, and the
gentle Cynthia even went so far as to
conclude that D'Arcy might have a few
redeeming attributes.

Venturing to suggest it one morning, as
they stood shivering over the big fire in
the book-room (they had just come in
from a brisk walk, with noses red and
blood a-tingle), Pamela broke out impatiently: "Oh, when are we to be rid of
that insufferable Irish dandy?"

"We might change lodgers and fare
worse," rejoined Cynthia, stoutly.

"I can hardly conceive of it," answered
Pamela, smothering a yawn in her huge
muff.

"You evidently forget the Hessians."

Pamela's shoulders rose in a shrug of
disgust. "Ugh! Don't mention those
creatures," she said.

"And yet it was the Irish dandy that
saved us from them," went on the devil's
advocate, "and at peril of his life too."

"Pshaw!" said Pamela, tapping the
fender impatiently.

"You are unkind, Pamela," Cynthia

114

pursued. "Didn't he fight both of those horrible men?"

"Oh, that was nothing; any man would have done the same. And he wasn't hurt," added Pamela, perversity holding her tight.

"No, but they were, and he came very near being court-martialed, as Mr. Davis told us." Cynthia was growing bold in her championship. Pamela laughingly drew her close and took her chin in her hand. "You dear little coz, are you going over to the enemy?" she asked, looking deep in the blue eyes.

"No, but I believe in giving the devil his due."

"Don't worry about the devil, dear, he will take care of his own."

"They have been very kind and considerate," said Cynthia, bound to make her point. "And Captain Gregory has helped Aunt Clarissa a great deal."

"I don't object to the doctor, his profession is a merciful one," Pamela replied, "but that coxcomb, Major D'Arcy, with his fine London airs, and his redcoats, drives me to a frenzy. And that brogue!'' she added, comically putting her fingers to her ears. "Oh, that brogue!''

Cynthia had to laugh. "It should plead for him," she cried, merrily. "It's not English."

"No, but it's British,'' rejoined Pamela.

"You're relentless."

"As long as we are prisoners," Pamela said, firmly.

"Well, it won't last forever," assured her cousin.

"The day they evacuate the city, I shall begin to like them; when they sail for England I shall adore them," answered Pamela.

"A fine way to love your enemies," answered Cynthia.

"The most beautiful in the world, dear; at a distance," said Pamela; and the controversy dropped.

Strangely enough, the first of a curious concatenation of small events that were destined to modify somewhat Miss Towneshend's stringent opinion of the young officer, took place not many moments after the conversation just chronicled. They were still standing before the fire gazing pensively at the leaping blaze, when a low knock at the door, leading to what they called their part of the house, roused them from their revery. In answer to Pamela's summons, the kinky head and black face of Sambo was thrust cautiously in, and after rolling his eyes mysteriously about the room for a second, he tiptoed toward them.

"A letter for you, Miss Pamela," said the old darkey, mysteriously, and Pamela reached for it with wonder in her eyes.

"It's from Ned, Cynthia!" she cried joyfully, ripping the folded ends from their pressure of wax.

"From Ned?" gasped Cynthia, springing to her side.

"Yes. Who left it, Sambo?"

"A farm-boy gave it to Cicely at the gate, Miss Pamela, and went right off."

But Pamela heard not a word of the explanation; her eyes were rapidly scanning the letter's contents.

"What does he say, Pamela?" asked Cynthia, in an ecstasy of suspense.

"All is well; he is coming," answered

117

Pamela, reading on swiftly. "You may go, Sambo. Thank you."

"Is Massa Eddy well, Miss Pamela?" ventured the old servitor.

"Yes, Sambo, very," and Sambo went out thanking "the Lord" for the safe-keeping of his dear young master.

The door had scarce clicked behind him when Cynthia burst out: "Quick, dear Pamela, read to me; it is cruel to keep me in suspense."

The letter had evidently been written in the greatest haste, and Pamela read slowly: "Dearest Sis: I have just a chance of getting word through to you. I only write to say, that I hope to be with you as soon as this. I shall leave the camp before daybreak to-morrow morning——"

"That's to-day," interrupted Cynthia, eagerly.

"So it is," answered Pamela, glancing at the date.

"Please read on. You are so slow," said the impatient Cynthia. So impatient were they both, and so eagerly interested, that neither of them heard the door at their backs open.

118

"I shall leave the camp before daybreak to-morrow morning, disguised as——" There was a cough behind them, and the girls whirled to face the intruder, Pamela crushing the note in her hand.

"I beg your pardon, ladies," said Gregory, his old face a blank to the quick, questioning scrutiny of Pamela, who wondered, in a tremble, if he had heard.

"Good morning, Captain Gregory," she said, quietly.

"Good morning to you, Miss Towne· shend, and to you, Miss Deane," said the old doctor. "I hope I don't intrude?"

"Oh, not at all," said Cynthia, flurried.

"We are hugging the fire, after our walk," Pamela remarked.

"It's a bitter day," said Gregory. "I trust your mother is well this morning," he added.

"Very, thank you, doctor. We are going to her now. Come, Cynthia." She lifted her muff from a chair, and they moved toward the door.

"I am driving you away."

"Oh, no, indeed; we were just going when you entered," said Cynthia, smiling.   As for Pamela, she could gather nothing from Gregory's wrinkled phiz, and she passed out of the room in a small panic.

Her perturbation would have been sensibly increased if she could have seen the doctor, a moment later, stoop and pick up the crumpled letter, which had slid through her muff to the floor, at the very instant of exit.

CHAPTER XI

Gregory smoothed out the wrinkled paper, which had adjusted itself to its original folds, and read the superscription. The writing was strong and masculine, and the old man had recourse to his snuff-box several times, as with speculative eyes he examined and re-examined the quill strokes. The more he pondered the less he could make out of it, and he was glad when D'Arcy appeared a few moments later.

"Not gone out yet, Greg?" he asked, stepping to where the old man stood.

"No, I am trying to thaw out," answered Gregory. "This is a devilish cold climate."

"I believe these damned Americans could make it warm enough for us if we gave 'em a show."

"Well, they'll soon have the chance," replied the doctor, referring to a secret

121

plan that was on foot, and which shall be told of later. Then he added: "I saw your divinity but a moment before you came in."

"She was here?" asked D'Arcy eagerly, turning from the fire.

"Yes," said the doctor, drily, "and curiously occupied."

"What do you mean?"

"She was reading what I judged to be a love-letter," answered Gregory.

"A love-letter, man!" ejaculated D'Arcy, for the moment losing his accustomed poise. "How do you know? Whom was she reading to?"

"As I entered the room," said the doctor, "Miss Towneshend and her cousin were standing where you stand, with their backs to me. I happened to overhear these words, which Miss Towneshend read from a letter: 'I shall leave the camp before daybreak to-morrow, disguised as——' Then I thought it time to discover myself."

"That was all you heard?" asked the Irishman, slowly.

"All," replied Gregory.

There was silence for a moment, then D'Arcy broke into an uneasy laugh. "Ah, you're suspicious by nature, Greg, like all Englishmen," he said. "The note was to Miss Deane."

"I happen to know differently. Here *is* the billet doux. Miss Towneshend dropped it as she went out."

Gregory held it out, and D'Arcy eagerly snatched it, reading the address again and again, with a sort of fascination.

"And what did you hear, Gregg?" he asked, finally.

"I heard Miss Towneshend read this much," and Gregory repeated, " 'I shall leave camp before daybreak to-morrow disguised as——' "

"And why the devil didn't you wait to hear how the blackguard was going to disguise himself?" cried D'Arcy.

"You hold the key to the mystery in your hand," replied the doctor, quietly.

"Greg, I wouldn't have thought it of you," said the other, reproachfully.

"But you would have had me eavesdrop for your personal satisfaction," rejoined Gregory.

"Forgive me, old man. I'm not myself," said the youngster, going to him.
"What do you make of it?" he added,
holding the troublesome piece of paper out
at arm's length.

"Honest?" questioned Gregory, watching his friend narrowly.

"Honest," answered D'Arcy.

"I think," said the doctor, deliberately formulating his opinion, even to
himself, for the first time. "I think
that the fair Miss Towneshend is
particularly interested in some one in
the rebel camp at Valley Forge, who
intends getting through the lines to pay
her a visit."

"Faith, the gentleman will never return
alive to Valley Forge if I clap eyes on
him," said the Major, with his peculiar
little smile.

"Well, he evidently hasn't arrived yet,
or they wouldn't have been reading his
letter so eagerly."

"You break my heart, Greg," cried
D'Arcy. "Was she really reading the
scoundrel's letter eagerly?"

"Not so *very* eagerly, Jack," said the

doctor, attempting to ameliorate the rigor of his former remark.

"Thank you for that," answered Jack. "You give me a crumb of comfort," and he looked so dispirited that Gregory felt for him.

"Brace yourself, Jack," he said. "We must improve that heart action, eh, lad?"

"Faint heart will never do, will it, Greg?" said D'Arcy.

"Not for so fair a lady, Jack," and the doctor clapped him on the shoulders, buoyantly, and with an air of confidence that was tremendously reassuring to his companion, the complexion of whose variable spirits was easily changed.

"Egad, Greg!" he cried, "you have a soul above pill boxes and lancets, after all."

"Ah, you rascal, what would your mother say to a rebel daughter-in-law?" the doctor laughed, pleased at the turn in his humor.

"Faith, that's the kind every mother has to put up with," answered D'Arcy, sparkling.

"I think her ladyship would prefer one English bred, though," ventured Gregory.

"I've written and told her of Pamela," said the Irishman, simply.

"What!" exclaimed the Captain. "You've written to Lady D'Arcy?"

"Three weeks ago," announced the young man, tersely.

"Well, now I do believe you're in earnest," said the doctor. "Even in the palmy days at Bath with Lady Betty Kew, you never wrote to your mother."

"Don't be teasing me, Greg. They were calf days."

"You wanted to call me out for saying that very same thing," replied the old man, smiling.

"Dear old Greg, did I want to fight you?" asked the Major, affectionately.

"You did indeed. But I must be off." He threw his big cloak about him and drew on his gloves. On the threshold he turned and said: "Don't forget to tell Miss Towneshend there will be a little company of officers here to-morrow night, and that they must not be disturbed."

"It's too much like giving orders to a queen," said D'Arcy.

"But you must, Jack. The plan of

attack is to be given out, and there must be absolutely no interruption."

"I know, I know," answered the Major, gloomily.

"I'll tell her myself, if you'd rather."

"No, no," interposed D'Arcy, hastily. A poor excuse to speak with her was better than none to him. "I'll go to her at once," he added.

"Good" said Gregory, and he went out.

D'Arcy's "at once" stretched over five minutes, during which he stood gazing at the letter, which he still held in his hand. It puzzled and discomfited him. The thought of a rival had never crossed his mind, and he was now inwardly cursing at the folly, that could have hoaxed him into thinking, that so fair a creature as Pamela could have wasted her sweetness upon a townful of unsusceptible provincial gallants. He could have withstood her silent, haughty dislike and disdain, fortifying himself with hope; but the young Irishman was too much of a man of the world, and possessed too keen a knowledge of women, to doubt that this peerless one, upon whom his heart was set, would ever plight herself lightly. If she loved once, those eyes and that proud mouth told him, she would love forever, and he was filled with a sort of numb despair.

He pulled himself together with an effort and moved toward the door. His hand was outstretched for the knob, when it opened and Pamela rushed almost into his arms.

"I beg ten thousand pardons, Miss Towneshend," he said, bowing.

"The fault was mine," she answered, recovering herself. Her eyes avoided his, and glanced quickly about the floor of the room.

"You are searching for something?" he asked, almost timidly.

"Yes. I dropped a letter, I think, when I was here a while ago."

"May this chance to be it?" said D'Arcy, holding it out.

The crimson flew to her cheeks for a moment, then she said quite steadily: "Yes, that is it. It was very stupid of me."

"I was about to bring it to you. Captain Gregory picked it up."

"It was very kind of you." She had recovered her composure now, and was turning to leave him.

"Miss Towneshend," he said.

"Yes."

"May I speak with you one moment?"

"What is it?" she asked.

"A small company of officers is to meet here to-morrow night, and——" he hesitated.

"Yes." Her voice was as cold and colorless as ice.

"May we have a—a—undisturbed possession of this room?" stammered D'Arcy.

"You mean that you will require the household to retire early?" she asked.

"You interpret my request harshly, Miss Towneshend."

"I save you that trouble," answered the girl, and there was that in her voice and look which called quick protest from him.

"Believe me, Miss Towneshend, if it will in any way inconvenience you, I will do my best to have the rendezvous changed."

She felt the remonstrance, but the anger

deep in her, refused to let her see the
young officer's gentle intention. The
deferential, almost humble, figure before
her, brought nothing but a full consciousness of his being an intruder; badged with
his coat of scarlet, he represented to her
all that was hateful and despicable.

"Major D'Arcy," she said, in a low
voice, "you and your companions in arms
have occupied Philadelphia, now for near
three months. Every day of that occupation has been a source of inconvenience
and bitterness to all loyal Americans in the
town. I don't complain; it's all the fortune of war. But it is no kindness to me
to mask your demands under guise of
courteous request."

"You wrong my intention, Miss Towneshend," he said, feelingly, humiliated, that
this girl, of all girls, should so misunder-
stand him.

"I have no wish," she answered, "to
profit by any special consideration on your
part."

"You make me ashamed of my uniform,
Miss Towneshend."

"Every British officer should have

broken his sword rather than have turned it against people of his own blood, fighting justly," burst out Pamela, passionately.

"You speak from the heart," he said, and he could feel himself all of a quiver.

"That is where I feel," she answered.

And then with some unaccountable emotional impulse, D'Arcy felt every trace of reserve swept from him. He knew only that the girl he loved stood before him, defiant, cold, hard; and he felt irresistibly that he must tell her, must show her, how he felt.

"I would give my sword—or break it gladly, for some small place there," he said, with a tremor in his voice, while his eyes met hers, straight and compellingly.

"Major D'Arcy!" she exclaimed, scornfully, her eyes blazing into his. Then she moved away, but he stood in front of the door. There was something of her own defiance and resentment in his face now, but his voice pleaded for him.

"Don't turn away, Miss Towneshend. No girl need be afraid of a tale of honest love. And—and," he faltered, "I have such a tale to tell.'

"I cannot listen to you. Let me pass," she cried.

"I must speak, Miss Towneshend," he said, quietly, and for the moment she felt herself powerless under his intensity. "Ever since that autumn morning three months ago, when I came into your garden, and saw you standing like some lovely flower, I have loved you. Don't shrink from me; it's no crime for a man to bend to the fragrance of a rose, and my lips would prove recreant to my heart if they refused longer to speak."

"Major D'Arcy," she answered, with a sort of breathlessness, "you take advantage of your position in this house to speak in a manner that you must know is distasteful to me."

"God forgive you, Miss Towneshend, for doubting my motives. I could stand your indifference to the little I have to offer—my life: as much as any man could give; but your scorn humbles me beyond the telling, showing, as it does, how little you understand what I wish."

"I could not desire to understand what you wish," answered the girl, recovering herself somewhat, "and as for doubting your motives, an American woman has no other alternative. To be loyal to her country, she must be loyal to herself; an enemy to one is an enemy to both; and I beg of you, if you are what common report credits you with being—a gentleman by birth and breeding—that you will never refer again to a subject that can but be painful to us both."

Her words were like lashes in the face of the man, and when she had finished every muscle was strung tight, and his face was set like a mask.

"I trust Miss Towneshend will pardon my indiscretion," he said. "I have the honor to bid you good morning," and bowing very low, he turned toward the door, throwing his cloak about him as he went.

"This apartment will be quite at your service to-morrow evening, as you request," said Pamela.

"Thank you," he said, and bowing once more he passed out, and she heard the big hall door shut after him. A moment later she could see him through the window, bending against the wind, pass down the gardens.

CHAPTER XII

A VISITOR

The girl stood quite still, just where he left her. Her mind was in a tumult, and she had an overwhelming sense of let-down; she had braced herself for a climax, and it hadn't come off. The enemy had retreated ignominiously, but she had none of the inspiring elation of victory. There was a something in his voice too, that still rang in her ears, and she would never, to her dying day, forget the look in those eyes. Did the victory really belong to her? was the question with which she tortured herself. Before she had chance to answer, in a way that would satisfy her vanity, she was summarily interrupted by the quick entrance of Cynthia, whose face was aglow.

"Oh, he's come, Pamela, he's come!" she gasped.

"Ned!" cried Pamela, casting intro-spection to the winds.

"Yes, he's here."

"Where?"

Cynthia turned to the open door for answer, and called down the passage: "Ned, it's all right. Come."

A moment later she was in his arms, her flaming face against his cold cheek.

"Ned!" was all she could murmur.

"Sis, dear, here I am. You got my note?"

"Not half an hour ago," said Cynthia, hovering about, a light in her eyes.

"You should have brought it yourself," said Pamela, gayly, standing off to survey him, her eyes taking in every detail of his disguise, from the stout shoes and woolen stockings to the rough great-coat that enveloped him.

"It would have been safer," he laughed. "I had a hard time getting through. The roads are more carefully guarded than before. I thought they were after me once, but I gave 'em the slip."

"It was dangerous venturing by day," said Pamela.

"It would have been worse by night. How is mother?"

136

"I'll go and tell her you are here. She couldn't stand having you burst in on her," said Cynthia, and she was off like a flash, to be back the quicker.

The brother and sister, left alone, had a thousand questions, treasured through the long weeks, and the talk was fast. Answers came through the glance of an eye or the pressure of hand. They filled the precious minutes to the brim, with all that the long absences denied them.

"And do your lodgers give you any trouble?" he asked, after a while. "Are they well-behaved and considerate?"

"They are models, Ned," she answered, "and are really a great protection for us."

"That Irish Major, what's his name? Does he behave civilly and treat you with respect?"

"He's very nice—for a red-coat," said Pamela.

"I have heard as much."

"You have heard of him?" she questioned, and the interest with which she asked it, astonished herself.

"Yes," said Towneshend. "Curiously enough, the young Marquis de Lafayette, whom I told you about, met him in Paris several years ago, and speaks very highly of him.''

"Tell me, what did he say?" She could have bitten through her wayward tongue, and her cheeks were playing her false, too.

"Oh, he said he was once on the British embassy at Paris, and was a son of Lord D'Arcy."

"Is that all?" she asked.

The obtuseness of a brother was hardly proof against the disappointment in her voice.

"See here!" he cried, taking her hands and laughing out. "The Major hasn't been recruiting in the household, has he?"

"What do you mean?" she asked, with wonder-wide eyes, repairing her defenses.

"The red-coat is not proving too attract-ive, eh, Sis?"

"You stupid boy. If you but knew how I despised him!" she said, and convinced him thoroughly—and almost herself.

The banter went on. Their spirits rose joyously, only at their height to be plunged into terror, not many minutes later.

It was the alert ear of the young officer that caught the sound of tramping feet.

"What was that?" he cried sharply, springing up.

"What?" questioned Pamela, the note of concern in his voice gripping her.

"I thought I heard something."

"Your imagination, dear," she said, as he stepped to the window. He held the curtains aside for an instant, and then jumped back with an oath.

"Imagination, the devil, Pamela! Do you see those red-jackets going around the corner of the house?"

"Soldiers?" gasped the girl. "Where?"

She was answered by Cynthia, who at that moment burst into the room, fear in every line of her face.

"Ned, Ned!" she cried, "the house is surrounded! What are we to do?"

Disciplined in danger, once the first shock of surprise had swept over him, the young officer had himself well in hand. No one knew better his fate, if captured, and his calmness surprised even the two girls who knew his iron restraint.

"I felt that I hadn't thrown 'em off

the track," he said quietly, drawing a pistol from his pocket. "I must make a run for it."

"It would be folly," cried Pamela. "They would shoot you down before you had gone ten steps."

"I can't be taken," said the young officer, grimly. "I am within the enemy's lines disguised. That means——"

"Ssh!" murmured Cynthia, putting her hand over his mouth to push back the horrid word. "What shall we do, Pamela?"

"There is only one thing to do," answered the girl. "Come this way," she said, and moved toward the door across the room.

"Where?" he questioned, doubtfully, but following.

"The old spare chambers," answered Pamela. "Major D'Arcy and Captain Gregory occupy them. Find mother, Cynthia," she said, turning to her cousin, "and see that she is not alarmed."

With a cry, the girl threw herself in Towneshend's arms.

"There, there, dear," he said, gently, "I'll outwit them yet."

"I'm afraid," she sobbed.

"Come," said Pamela, holding open the door. "They will not enter here, if I can help it."

"They will never take me if they do," said Towneshend, quietly, and he gripped his pistol significantly.

"No, no, not that," pleaded Cynthia.

"Go, Cynthia, dear," said Pamela, and the girl shrank from the room.

"I will stand guard here," went on Pamela. "My wits will keep them at bay, I think."

"What a home-coming is this, Sis!" answered the lad, lingering. But with a hasty kiss, she pushed him in, closed the door, and turning the key, put it in her pocket. She scarce had time to shift her position to the front of the fire, when the door on the opposite side of the room was flung open, and a sergeant with a file of men marched in.

The girl, tremulous, and fear-stricken within, held her head high, and swept the intruders with an indignant glance. "What is the meaning of this intrusion?"

she asked, as the file drew up and the sergeant stepped forward.

"A rebel spy has been traced to this house. Have orders to search every apartment," said the man, curtly.

"There are no apartments on this side of the house," answered Pamela.

"Where does that door lead?" he questioned, stepping across the room.

"Oh, there is a suite of chambers there, but they are occupied," said the girl, her heart pounding, but showing no trace of it in the carefully-steadied voice.

"It's locked," the sergeant said, trying the door.

"I suppose so," said Pamela.

"Where is the key?"

"One might imagine the occupant would have it." She was struggling for time desperately.

"We'll have the door down, Corporal," he said, and one of the grenadiers stepped forward.

"I doubt if Major D'Arcy will care for that," she remarked, quietly, so quietly that it sounded to herself like a far-away whisper.

"Major who?" questioned the sergeant, sharply.

"Major D'Arcy, of the Grenadier Guards."

"Is he quartered here?" asked the man, suspiciously.

"I have said so," she answered.

"Why is the door locked?"

"Major D'Arcy is at headquarters and will no doubt give you any information you require—and perhaps even the keys."

There was hurried whispering between the corporal and sergeant, while hope struggled feebly to rise in her; only to be dashed back a moment later, when the sergeant said gruffly: "We'll go in, any-how."

"As you please," replied Pamela, firmly, though her lip quivered and she could feel her knees bend under her.

She couldn't have told the time that passed, her mind seemed stretched across eternity; she was conscious of seeing the broad red shoulders shoved against the door, which resisted stoutly, then like a flash the door to the hall banged open, and D'Arcy strode in.

"What is this?" he cried, looking about the room, and the anger in his voice was savage.

"We are on the track of a rebel spy, Major," answered the astounded sergeant, "and Captain Dacier has ordered us to search the house."

"I am very sorry, Miss Towneshend, that you have been subjected to this annoyance," said D'Arcy, turning to the girl.

"Pray, Major D'Arcy, don't consider me in the matter. Yours would have been the annoyance."

"Mine?" he questioned, puzzled.

"They were about to break into your chambers."

"Is the door locked?" asked D'Arcy, in surprise.

"It is locked," answered Pamela, steadily, and her eyes held him.

"The lady said you would know why it was locked, sir, and that you had the key."

D'Arcy didn't appear to hear, his face never moved from that of the girl's before him, but he answered sharply: "Quite

right, Sergeant. You may withdraw
your men to the gardens.''

"Yes, sir,'' answered the man, saluting.
"What shall I tell the captain?''

"That I wish to see him here.''

"Yes, sir.''

There was a quick word of command,
the rattle of arms, and the squad melted
from the room, leaving the two face to
face.

CHAPTER XIII

MISTAKEN IDENTITY

For Pamela the harder task remained, and as she stood there with clenched hands, a sense of futility and powerlessness overcame her, and she knew that her nerve was gone; in a moment the whole secret would be his, as part of it was already, and she would be crying for mercy to the man who not an hour before had been at her feet. She would have borne the tortures of the rack rather than beg for herself; but for him, Ned, her brother, any abasement, rather than that he should suffer. Was this cold, self-possessed man standing before her the same gracious, half-timid, suppliant person who had pled with her? Would he listen? Would he believe her oath, that her Ned was not a spy?

The agony of these and a hundred other doubtful questions fluttered her mind, and showed in her face, and every gentle, pitying instinct in D'Arcy felt for her. And yet feeling seemed dead within him. She was fighting for the man she loved, and Chance had chosen him for her antagonist. He, of all persons in the world, was bidden to save or destroy her lover, and either way to destroy himself. The grim irony of it forced a smile to his lips, and seeing it she spoke, stepping toward him and holding out the key.

"Thank you," she said.

"He is there?" asked D'Arcy, mechanically.

"I swear to you he is not a spy," she burst out, passionately.

"You love him?" he said.

"As my life!" she cried. "I throw myself on your generosity. Appearances are against him, I know; he is disguised, but it was only his eagerness to get here, only that."

"I can understand," he replied, but there was no interest in his voice; he spoke in a dull monotone. He knew how this girl could love, if she ever did love; the thought of it had haunted him all these weeks past, and now he, who had

dreamed dreams, was awakened to what?
To the bitter reality, that it was not
for him. Should it be for that other
hiding there, whose fate he held in his
hand?

She could see the struggle in him.
"Don't give him up," she cried. "He's
too young to die, and they would hang
him. Oh, God, can't you see it would
break my heart? Have some pity."

"Miss Towncshend, can you swear on
your honor that he is not within our lines
to seek information?" he asked.

"I swear it," said Pamela.

His eyes seemed to touch her soul, and
he knew that she spoke truth.

"I exceed my authority," he said, "but
I will save him if I can."

"I thank you," said Pamela, humbly.

"Don't," he murmured. "My reward
is that light in your eyes. Take this
key," he added. "I must go to Dacier.
I will return in a moment." And he
hurried out.

Captain Dacier had but just received his
message from the sergeant and was coming toward the house. They met on the

steps, and D'Arcy's salute was of the coolest.

"Sergeant Trip informed me that you wanted to see me," said the Captain.

"Yes," said the Major, "he was quite unwarrantably trying to force his way into my apartments."

"But there is a spy in the house."

"I doubt it," said D'Arcy, curtly. "You have searched thoroughly?" he asked.

"Almost entirely," answered Dacier.

"Well, my rooms were locked, and I have the key."

"He must be somewhere," replied the Captain, nettled.

"Must he?" questioned D'Arcy, quizzically.

"There is some mystery," said the other.

"Clear it up, by all means," said D'Arcy. "I accept entire responsibility for any spy being in the house," he added.

"I shall report the whole affair to head-quarters," Dacier said, sharply.

"They don't like mysteries at headquarters, Captain Dacier. Good morning."

"Good morning, sir."

The Captain turned on his heel muttering, and D'Arcy, standing there, watched the company of Grenadiers file out, a moment later, into the road.

He turned back into the house, but his moment of Quixotic enthusiasm had passed, and it was listlessly that he again entered the library. His cheeks tingled at the sight which met his eyes. She might have spared him that, was the thought that dashed through his head, as he saw her standing with her arms around the neck of a great-coated figure, that towered above her.

"It is Major D'Arcy," she cried joyously, turning to him. "Ned, he saved you. Major D'Arcy," she said, "I wish to present my brother, Captain Towneshend."

"Your *brother?*" gasped the Irishman, doubt and delight struggling hard to get the better of him. "Miss Towneshend, do you mean to tell me that it is your brother I have saved?"

"No other," said Pamela. "Who else could he have been?"

"He could have been the man I would have hated most in the world," answered D'Arcy, radiant. "Captain Towneshend," he said, stepping to the dragoon with outstretched, welcome hand, "it is a privilege to meet you, sir."

"I don't know how you accomplished it," said Towneshend, grasping the other's hand, "but I am mightily obliged to you."

"And I," said Pamela, looking at him curiously, "can never tell you." She put out her hand, and D'Arcy took it gently to his lips, the blood surging at mad pace to his head.

It was late in the afternoon, as dusk was falling, that D'Arcy and Towneshend rode away from the house, and they had ridden some miles before the British officer, bidding his companion good-bye and God-speed, turned his own horse in the direction of the town. The stars twinkling frostily on him, as he sped, had a new message for him that night, and Hope was the burden of it.

Supping at mess later, he was the life of the whole table, reminiscent of the old-time D'Arcy; sparkling, witty, flippant, and gay. His jests bubbled and overflowed, swamping the youngsters in exuberant joy, and the oldsters too, for that matter, though their satisfaction was less ebullient.

He tore himself away early, however, for he was not unmindful of certain awkward questions which might arise from Dacier's representations, at headquarters, of the morning's happenings. Piquet till midnight with the chief, and an incidental loss of thirty or forty guineas, set that right though, if it really needed any adjustment; for my Lord Cornwallis had a special liking for his dashing, good-humored aide.

Gregory, slippered and drowsy, in front of the fire, was struggling valiantly to keep his pipe-bowl hot when D'Arcy came in. They had not met since early morning, and the old man was eager to hear the Major's budget of news. News he had, the doctor was quite sure, as he watched him unbuckle sword and cloak, but he

was wise enough to wait for it, and let it
come as it would. Glasses were filled and
D'Arcy called the toast: "To the fairest
maid in all the world."

"With all my heart, Jack. The little
rebel?"

"Egad, Greg, she's a loyal rebel. I
adore her. She gave me her hand——"

"What!" said the doctor, sitting up
straight. "She gave you her hand?
Have you asked her to marry you already?"

"Of course I asked her," said D'Arcy,
"and she refused me with the air of the
duchess that she is."

"But you just said she gave you her
hand," Gregory said, puzzled.

"Oh, you silly old Greg. That was
afterward, and she gave it to me to kiss."

"Little baggage!" ejaculated the doctor.
"Jack, she's trifling with you."

"That's the point, Greg," answered
D'Arcy, gaily. "It's me she's trifling
with—and no one else—mind that."

"What's become of t'other fellow, the
mysterious man of disguise?" questioned
the old man, hopelessly at sea.

"Ah, he's a jewel, Greg. I could love

him as a brother—if I had the chance," laughed the Irishman.

"You saw him?"

"I did, indeed."

"Where?"

"Here. He spent most of the afternoon with his sweetheart, and at five o'clock I gave him my company for five miles, on his way back to the rebel camp."

"I give it up, Jack," said the doctor. "You're either out of your head or talking riddles."

"If you'd not be interrupting every second, Captain Gregory, I could tell a straightforward tale; and a very pretty one it is."

"Go on, I'll not stop you."

"I'll begin at the end," began D'Arcy.

"As usual," the doctor couldn't help putting in.

D'Arcy drew a deep puff from his pipe, and kept silent for a couple of minutes, to punish him. Then he went on: "Well, his sweetheart is not mine, Greg."

"I can readily believe that."

"Oh, you stupid old Greg! You don't mean what I mean."

"What do I mean?" asked the doctor.

"You mean that we are both in love with the same girl. And so we are," he added, "but in a different way."

"And you compromised on that basis, did you, Jack?" asked Gregory, with deep irony.

"Yes, I was perfectly satisfied with his way; he's her brother, Greg."

"Her *brother!*" ejaculated Gregory.

"No less—and thank heaven, no more," answered the Irishman.

"And pray, who is *his* sweetheart?"

"Why, his cousin, Miss Cynthia, you blockhead."

"It's like one of Mr. Garrick's comedies, Jack."

"It's better; it's real," said D'Arcy.

"But why did she give you her hand to kiss, if she wouldn't give it to you to keep?" questioned Gregory.

"You know not the ways of women, Greg. Your flinty heart has never been touched by experience."

"Your experience with 'em seems to

have been of much value to you, Jack," answered the other, with a snort.

"Faith, Greg, every woman is a new experience."

"It's a long lesson," answered the old man, dubiously.

"But a pleasant one, and always worth the learning."

"You should know; you've been constantly at school," said the doctor.

"And my latest school-mistress is the best," cried D'Arcy.

"Because she's given you a harder task," laughed Gregory. "The rest were too eager for that fastidious dandy, Jack D'Arcy."

"Out of the mouths of babes and fools! Faith, Greg, you speak wisdom. You've summed up the whole philosophy of love: what we can't have, we want; and we flout whatever shows us favor."

"It's an ungallant philosophy," puffed the old man.

"Ah, philosophy has no manners at all, Greg."

"Which brings us back to the statement that Miss Towneshend allowed you to kiss her hand."

"It was gratitude, Greg; but it was sweeter than any other woman's favor."

"Gratitude?"

"I saved her brother," said D'Arcy. "Dacier had a file of the Guards here, and they would have strung him up as sure as they would have laid hands on him. I threw 'em off the scent."

"What if he was really a spy?" questioned Gregory, with concern.

"She swore he wasn't."

"Naturally," grunted the doctor.

"Have you ever looked in her eyes, Greg?" asked the young man.

"No, I haven't."

"You'd never doubt her word if you had."

"I'd never look in a woman's eyes for the truth," answered the doctor.

"I know that, Greg. Truth is a will-o'-the-wisp, and eludes all such crabbed old bachelors as yourself."

"But was it discretion?" asked the old man.

"No. It was love," answered D'Arcy, and Gregory saw that he was proof against any subtle casuistry.

"If the lady refused your suit, why are you so happy to-night?" he asked.

"Because I was able to serve her."

"You still have hope?" questioned the doctor.

"I have," answered D'Arcy.

"Well," said Gregory, leaning over and clapping him on the back, "you deserve her, Jack, and may you win her."

"She'll never have me as long as I wear a red coat," laughed the Irishman.

"Damme, get a bottle-green one then, or any color that the wench wants," exclaimed the doctor, testily.

"If I come out of to-morrow's scrimmage whole, Greg, I'll sell out," said D'Arcy.

"Fudge!"

"I mean it," went on the Major. "If she won't listen to a soldier, she may listen to a civilian."

"If you give up your sword, Jack, she'll want it back. The sex is wayward."

"Then she shall have it. Her wish is law to me."

"Well, let's sleep on it," said Gregory, rising. And they did; the one soundly,

the other fretfully, dreaming dreams once
more. While neither had prevision of
the calamity that was to fall on the morrow.

CHAPTER XIV

A COUNCIL OF WAR

Two young people under the Towneshend roof opened their eyes the following
morning on a new world. To Pamela,
early awake, but lying in her chintzed,
four-posted bed, long beyond the housewife's hour, the consciousness of it was
obscure, though in full possession of her.
She strove to see the events of the day
before, in rightful sequence, first forward,
then back, only to be baffled time and
again by the inconsequent obtrusion in
her mind, of a gallant, scarlet-coated
figure, that dominated the whole, and
refused to be banished. It irritated her;
she was restless and uncomfortable; new
conditions seemed to have arisen in the
night to surround and hem her in.
Something, she knew not what, curbed the
joyous sense of freedom and personal independence in which she gloried—*and he
had kissed her hand.* With a flush, she

remembered that she had given it to him
for that purpose. "And why not?" she
cried, petulantly, pulling the bell-cord to
summon her maid. There was no answer
to her question, and Cicely was well
chidden, on her appearance, for tardiness.

In fact, she was a willful mistress that
morning, and changed places with her
usually dominating little handmaiden.
An unsatisfactory half hour was spent
before the mirror in futile attempts at
hair dressing, that would not go right.
Then frock after frock, and ribbon after
ribbon was tossed aside, and the morning
was well advanced when Cynthia, enter-
ing the room, found both her cousin and
Cicely in tears. So disturbing is the
boundary crossing into an undiscovered
country.

Pamela kept in the far parts of the house
all day; away from the book-room, and
any possibility of chance meeting.

With D'Arcy it was different. A
man's processes are simpler, his transitions
and adaptations swifter. At the first
glimpse of dawn, he grew restless, and by
the time the sunshine twinkled through

the frosted panes, he was wide awake,
collecting scattered, hazy thoughts, to
explain a boundless elation. He called
through the open door to Gregory, sleep-
ing soundly, and called again, at no sign
of response.

"Eh, what? Did you call, Jack?"
answered the old man at last, starting up.

"I kissed her hand, Greg," shouted
D'Arcy.

"What? Kissed whose hand? What
the devil——" sputtered Gregory, and
then, as a merry laugh came through to
him, he flounced over indignantly and was
asleep, leaving the youngster to wonder
how such an epoch event in his life could
arouse so little interest in his companion.
The color of life for him had changed
suddenly, in hours, from somber to rose
tint, and he couldn't conceive that the
joy was all his. He demanded that the
whole world should be joyous and gay
with him and should share his happiness.
The prospect of the day and night's business before him cast a slight shadow, but
it passed, and when Gregory again awoke
it was to find him in full banter with his

servant, who was shaving and administering the other sacred rites of toilet.

It was a full day and busy among the conquerors. Headquarters was the center of galloping aides, regimental and brigade commanders. Sir William Howe had wakened up. News of the pitiable condition of Washington's little army, encamped on the frozen hills about Valley Forge, had determined the British commander to make a rapid night march, an early morning attack, sweep the miserable rebel remnant into oblivion, and end the war once for all. For fear of miscarriage, the project had been kept a profound secret, and though the rank and file felt intuitively that a movement was on foot, not even regimental commanders knew anything of its character or its object. It was intended that no inkling of the secret should leak out till just before starting, and to that purpose colonels and company officers had been ordered to report at different meeting-places to receive important instructions. Colonel Sir Edward Jennison, of the Guards, with his staff, was to rendezvous at the Towneshend

house, where D'Arcy was directed to bring
them full instructions and orders.

It was something after eight in the
evening that D'Arcy rapped on the
knocker of the outer door, and was ad-
mitted by Gregory. The company of
officers was already assembled, and
under guidance of the old doctor, had been
doing full justice to a copious bowl of
deliciously brewed punch, sent in by the
courtesy of Mistress Towneshend, as the
Captain whispered to Jack. It tasted
nectar to the Major on that account.
He was greeted uproariously and called
upon for a toast, but Sir Edward demanded business first, and D'Arcy pro-
ceeded to spread the table with road-maps,
plans, and orders for the night's work.
To keep them flat, he drew two silver-
mounted pistols from his coat to weight
the edges; the same memorable pistols
that had stood him in such good stead on
that far-away night when he and the
Marquis of G—— had ridden together.
By just such trivial expedients does tricky
Chance sweep a man's destiny aside.

He and Jennison were soon deep in

whispered consultation, the roomful of
men looking on with undisguised impatience. At last the Colonel spoke.

"Gentlemen," he said, "I know that
you all have a very pardonable curiosity
concerning the enterprise that is on foot,
and I have orders here from headquarters
that will not only satisfy your curiosity,
but gratify your pride."

"That's good," whispered Dalrymple,
the senior Major, audibly. "We've been
mortifying our pride long enough."

"If not your flesh, eh, Major?" said
Captain Dacier, under his breath.

"You're right, Major," said Jennison,
smiling, and then continued: "The Commander-in-Chief has thought secrecy of
the utmost importance in this instance,
and, therefore, no hint of the intended
movement has gotten out. It is his
intention to make this attack a complete
surprise to the enemy, and to that purpose these instructions have not been
given to regimental commanders till now."

"When do we move, sir?" questioned
Farquhar, an alert little captain. Sir
Edward, for answer, drew out his fob and

glanced at his watch. "It is half-after eight," he said, and then, reading from the orders before him, "The advance, composed of both regiments of the Guards, and the brigade of Hessians, is to move at one o'clock."

"To-morrow, sir?" asked Dacier.

"To-day—to-night, sir?" answered the Colonel, frowning. "You will have about four hours for preparation." Then he addressed the others, who had clustered about the table by which he was standing. "As you will see by the maps here, gentlemen," he said, "the enemy's position is a strong one."

"We'll sweep 'em off their feet," interjected Dalrymple.

"You talk as if the Guards were armed with brooms, Dal," laughed D'Arcy.

"The bayonet is a grenadier's broom, Jack," answered the big Major.

"Aye, sir," said Sir Edward, "and we'll give it to 'em. As I was saying," he went on, "the enemy holds a strong position, their intrenchments are strung along these hills, which are heavily timbered." His finger traced over the maps, and the little group about him followed with eager eyes. "At their back, you see, is the river."

"I don't envy 'em to-morrow morning's bath," said little Farquhar.

"That's just the point, Captain," answered the Colonel; over his shoulder. "We'll drive 'em into the river. Our regiment has the post of honor in the van," he continued, "and we must set the pace; we must prove ourselves worthy of the honor."

There were murmurs of approval all around, and, after studying the maps for a moment, he went on again. "The attack begins from this side with us. The Hessians move to the left, and the Eightieth, Forty-first and Ninety-second take the center." At this point Dalrymple leaned over to examine some detail of the plans, and he and the Colonel conversed in low tones for several minutes. The others drew back, and had resort to the decanters and punch-bowl, and took occasion to refill and put fire to their long pipe-stems.

"They are nothing but a disorganized

rabble, and if we hem 'em in so they can't run, they'll throw down their arms at once," remarked Dacier.

"Or drown like rats in the river," added Gregory.

"That's what they should do, Greg," said D'Arcy, who, with his back spread to the blaze on the andirons, was lazily blowing fragrant clouds toward the ceiling; "but," he added, "they won't. The beggars are sadly lacking in the knowledge of tactics, and don't know how to retreat, and as for their manual of arms, it gives 'em no information at all on the subject of throwing 'em down."

"You're right, Jack," put in Farquhar; "the rascals don't seem to know when they're beaten."

"Eh, what's that?" questioned the Colonel, overhearing the last phrase, and looking around. "Who said beaten?"

"I was saying, Colonel," answered Farquhar, "that the rebels never knew when they were beaten."

"Oh, the scoundrels can fight, damn 'em," exclaimed Jennison, "and they'll have to to-morrow."

"If everything goes right, it will end the war," said Dalrymple.

"Everything must go right," replied Sir Edward, positively. "This is the most important move we've made. There is no possible way in which our plans can have leaked out, and they'll be totally unprepared. We'll catch 'em napping, and rout 'em to the last man."

"They've only a handful fit for service, anyhow," said Dacier.

"That fox Washington seems to do most damage when he has only a band of disabled men. Remember Trenton and Princeton," rejoined Dalrymple.

"Oh, Dal, let's forget 'em," laughed D'Arcy.

"Yes," said Jennison, "they're like a bad dream."

"To-morrow we'll retrieve all that and wipe the score clean," muttered Farquhar, quaffing deep from the bowl's contents.

"We'll bring this Mr. Washington and his French aide, the Marquis de Lafayette, back to Philadelphia with us," exclaimed Dacier.

"I wonder if Frenchy is really a marquis?" asked Dalrymple.

"He's a beautiful marquis, Dal," replied D'Arcy, "and a charming gentleman. I knew him in Paris when he was only a lad."

"He must like the company he's keeping," remarked Dacier, sneeringly.

"A good fighting man is always good company, Captain Dacier," said D'Arcy, and he toised the Captain with a mocking eye.

Dacier flushed, and a retort was on his lips, when Dalrymple broke in heartily, "The best in the world, Jack."

And Sir Edward, who had not noticed the little incident, joined in commendation. "Sound doctrine that, gentlemen. And now," he added, turning to them all, "I think there is nothing more to be said. We'll all meet again before many hours."

"But who knows when or where we'll meet again after that, Sir Edward?" asked D'Arcy. "So sit ye down, and give us a toast."

The proposal was ' chorused by all assembled, and the Colonel found himself the center of brimming glasses. He held one himself, and he gave them, "The King, gentlemen; God bless him, and his fighting men!"

"The King and his fighting men," echoed the group.

"And may they always support one another," added Jennison, fervently.

"Forever!" shouted all.

"Fill again, Sir Edward. Boys, do your duty," cried D'Arcy, and when they had replenished, he lifted his glass, and gave the Commander-in-Chief and Lord Cornwallis.

"Here, here!" cried his companions "The Commander-in-Chief and Lord Cornwallis."

"That's hearty," said the Colonel, "and a good omen for the morrow. And now," he added, "I must bid you all good-night. You'd all best get a few hours' sleep before we start."

"Oh, Sir Edward, you can't go yet," exclaimed D'Arcy, taking him by the arm coaxingly. "Dal hasn't sung his song."

"That's so," said Farquhar.

"Come, Major," urged the others, "we
· must have it."

"What shall it be?" asked Dalrymple.

"That new song, Dal, about the little
dear in the alley," answered D'Arcy.

"Yes, that's the one," said Jennison,
seating himself and filling a pipe.

Dalrymple took a puff or two from his
"church warden," and then, with a "Here
goes, lads, don't forget the chorus," he
sang "Sally in Our Alley." It went with
a dash, and the choruses made the windows rattle, while Pamela and Cynthia,
not far away, shivered for fear of their
china and glass, which had been sent in
to honor the occasion. There was no
damage, however, save leakage, and the
decanters and bowl were at a low ebb,
when, at last, the Colonel staggered to his
feet determinedly.

"Jack D'Arcy, I see you're for a night
of it," he laughed.

"Only for a part of a night," answered
D'Arcy. "Drink and be merry, Colonel,
for to-morrow we—you know the rest,
Sir Edward. And if· we do, to-night
would have been wasted between sheets."

"You're a roisterer, Jack, and I'll leave you to your ways." He had buckled his cloak about him, and, turning to the others, who had risen, he bade them all good-night.

D'Arcy, picking up a candle, followed him out, and the frosty night air blew so refreshingly, after the heated, stuffy room, that he went down through the gardens with him. When he returned, they were roaring through another song, and D'Arcy took up the chorus with them:

> " Let the toast pass,
> Drink to the lass,
> I'll warrant she'll prove an excuse for the glass."

Then Dalrymple went on to the next verse:

> "Here's to the charmer whose dimples we prize,
> Now to the maid who has none, sir.
> Here's to the girl with a pair of blue eyes,
> And here's to the nymphs with but one, sir."

Again they rollicked through the chorus, and a final verse was demanded.

"For let 'em be clumsy and let 'em be slim,
Young or ancient, I care not a feather;
So fill a pint bumper quite up to the brim,
So fill up your glasses, way full to the brim,
And let us e'en toast them together."

sang Dalrymple, and they all joined in with:

"Let the toast pass,
Drink to the lass,
I'll warrant she'll prove an excuse for the glass."

There was a shout for more, but the big Major refused.

"You missed our last toast, D'Arcy," said Dacier.

"I hate to miss a good toast," said the Irishman. "We'll have it over again. What was it?"

"The ladies, Jack," answered Dalrymple.

"With all my heart! The ladies!" cried D'Arcy.

"May beauty and wit be always theirs," said Farquhar, enthusiastically.

"And may the sex complete be always ours," twinkled D'Arcy, raising his glass.

They were all about to drink, when

175

Dacier, whose capacity had been imposed upon woefully, interrupted.

"Now that Major D'Arcy is here," he said, "I would like to specialize my original toast, and propose the fair and charming young rebel, Miss Pamela Towneshend." There was just the slightest shade of insinuation in his voice, that sent a shiver up and down the backs of the others, to whom D'Arcy's interest was not a mystery. Dalrymple jumped into the breach hurriedly.

"Every one would gladly do homage to the beautiful and accomplished Miss Towneshend," he said, and Gregory, whose anxious eyes had been fastened on the face of his friend, breathed easier. He was premature, for Dacier, feeling a sort of challenge in Dalrymple's noticeable attempt to cover up his remark, snapped out in answer: "If they got a chance, yes; but D'Arcy keeps a good thing to himself."

"Oh, shut up," said Farquhar, fidgeting. But it had gotten beyond interference. Gregory saw that, and his heart sank.

"Captain Dacier, your taste is better than your manners," D'Arcy said, coldly, looking the Captain in the eyes.

"I shouldn't choose you for a judge of either, Major D'Arcy," retorted Dacier. He was still smarting at the morning's discomfiture, and his potations had brought it out fiercely. Gregory had stepped quickly to D'Arcy's side, and whispered, "For God's sake, mind yourself!"

D'Arcy either didn't hear, or didn't want to heed. He was conscious only of the smirking mouth before him, that had spoken trivially of her; he felt that he would like to crush it out of all semblance of anything human, and destroy the man, too. But this surge of feeling receded, and it was quite calmly and deliberately that he flung his glass of wine straight in the other's face.

'Damn you, D'Arcy," screamed the man, in a sputter, "I'll kill you."

"I meant to give you that opportunity," answered D'Arcy. "Do you consider yourself more proficient with a sword or a pistol?"

177

The rest of the little group had been
stunned by the rapidity and suddenness of
the whole thing, sitting agape as if at the
play, but now Dalrymple stepped angrily
between them.

"This affair must go no further," he
said.

"You're right, Major Dalrymple,"
chimed in Gregory, who was beside
himself at the turn things had taken.
"The reputation of the Guards is at
stake."

"Will Captain Dacier withdraw his very
impertinent and offensive remarks concerning a lady for whom I have the highest respect?" said D'Arcy.

"Of course, of course. Go ahead,
Dacier. Don't be a fool," urged fussy
little Farquhar.

"I'll be damned if I will," answered
Dacier.

"I'll be damned if you don't," cried
Dalrymple, out of all patience.

"Don't trust your salvation, Dal, to
anything so uncertain," said D'Arcy,
laughing.

"Jack, you'll ruin yourself, and make

her name a byword in the army, if this goes on,'' whispered Gregory.

"I'll kill the puppy who dared to slur her,'' was the answer he got. "Sir,'' D'Arcy went on, addressing Dacier, "you have the choice of weapons. We must go somewhere from the house, for I cannot risk annoying the regular inmates.''

"As you please,'' answered Dacier; "and I choose the rapier.''

"Very good,'' said D'Arcy.

"Gentlemen,'' here broke in Dalrymple again, "I will be no party to such a duel and I shall go straight to my Lord Cornwallis, if the matter isn't stopped. Captain Gregory and the others here will uphold me in my position.''

"We certainly will, Major,'' said Gregory.

"That would be most irregular,'' answered D'Arcy.

"Don't talk to me of irregularity, Jack,'' burst out Dalrymple. "When we are within four or five hours of an engagement, you want to go off shooting and stabbing on your own account, taking no heed of the honor of your regiment, which needs the help of every officer."

"I am perfectly willing to postpone the pleasure of meeting Captain Dacier till after to-morrow's engagement," replied D'Arcy.

"I am agreeable to Major D'Arcy's proposal," assented Dacier.

'That is satisfactory," said Dalrymple. "And if you're not killed to-morrow, you can kill one another when you get back," he added, bluntly.

"You put it crudely, Dal," remarked D'Arcy.

"I've no patience with either of you," answered Dalrymple, "and I'm going."

"It's time we were all abed," said Farquhar, making a move toward his hat and cloak.

"You're right, Captain," Gregory said, and the movement was general.

The good-nights had been said, and the party was about to leave the room, when Gregory, who was standing by the table, noticed that the maps and orders were still spread out. "Halloa!" he said.

"What is it?" asked Farquhar.

"The Colonel has left his papers," answered the doctor.

"It doesn't matter," said D'Arcy. "I'm going to headquarters about twelve; I'll take them with me."

"Just as well," said Dalrymple. "Good-night, Jack."

"I'll light you to the gate," said D'Arcy, taking up a candle.

"I am going up to bed," said Gregory.

"I'll be up in a few minutes, Greg," answered D'Arcy, as he followed the others out.

Gregory heard the bolts being shot back, and the door opened and shut behind them. He took up his candle, and mounted the stairs. The happenings of the night and the coming morning's desperate venture would have fallen out differently if he had but waited for the young Irishman's return.

CHAPTER XV

If Pamela shunned the book-room during the day, it was with bounding heart that she thought of it a hundred times. Late in the afternoon she quite brazenly proposed to Cynthia that they brew a punch, and send in the decanters of Madeira "as a compliment to Doctor Gregory and his guests of the evening." Cynthia was delighted with the disingenuous proposal, and half an hour before the company of officers assembled, Sambo had finished putting out the household's shining crystal—Pamela's pride—and the huge brimming bowl, flanked by choicest Madeira, and a dozen dusty bottles of sparkling Burgundy were placed on the glistening mahogany. The little housekeeper's heart fell as she surveyed the priceless array, but her cheeks glowed, and she was elated, nevertheless. She and Cynthia decided to sit up till the little

183

assembly dispersed; no careless house-wench could be trusted to remove the precious glass and china to the pantries, and even Sambo needed supervision. It must be confessed that they looked dubiously at one another, as the sound of song and laughter came to them, but they had the courage of their courtesy, and strengthened themselves against the sight of their treasure splintered and in pieces.

Sambo was on watch for the departure, and, as the officers filed out into the gardens, he called his young mistress and Cynthia, and the three tiptoed into the room. The air was heavy with smoke, through which a dozen candles flickered but dimly. The girls choked and coughed, but found relief in not a single broken glass.

Solicitude gave way to gaiety, and Sambo's tray was soon loaded with the precious weight.

He had left the room, and Cynthia was standing by the fire.

"I suppose the Major and Doctor Gregory have gone to bed," she said.

"I suppose so," answered Pamela, still

bustling about. She had come to the table, upon which lay the tell-tale orders and maps, still spread under the weight of D'Arcy's pistols. Leaning over, to get a glimpse, she read mechanically aloud, what met her startled eyes, "Plans of the American fortifications at Valley Forge."

"What?" asked Cynthia, listlessly, not hearing.

Pamela snatched up the paper, and read with widening eyes, her hands all of a tremor.

"Order of attack on Valley Forge, Cynthia!" she cried.

"What is it?" answered the girl, turning to her, startled.

"Look! It's a plot, Cynthia," and she read again, breathlessly, "Order of attack on Valley Forge; the advance composed of both regiments of the Guards, and the brigade of Hessians is to move at one o'clock."

"When?"

"It is dated Headquarters, December 29th," read Pamela.

"That's to-day," gasped Cynthia.

"They intend to attack to-night. It's a surprise," answered Pamela.

"What can we do?"

"Let me think, let me think," cried her cousin; but she couldn't think, thought seemed denied her; the heated, smoky room numbed her senses; her head was in a whirl. "They must have word," she murmured; "they must. I have it," she said, hurriedly, a moment later. "Quick, Cynthia! take Sambo to the stables and saddle Bess."

"What will you do, Pamela," asked the girl, trembling.

"I'll warn them," she answered.

"You would never get through," said Cynthia.

"I will get through," replied Pamela, firmly. She was herself again, well in hand, poised, determined. "I know every inch of the road, and can make it in two hours—three, at the most. If they are not warned, they'll be destroyed. Quick, dear, there is not a moment to spare."

"The mare will be ready in five minutes," cried Cynthia, caught by the enthusiasm. "Get a warm coat," she said, as she rushed from the room.

Once again Pamela turned to the table. She spread the order just as she had found it, and then read and re-read it, printing every word on her memory. She turned to go, and, seeing D'Arcy's cloak on the sofa, she threw it about her, and smiled as she saw herself in the mirror. One more look at the papers, and then—. She was bending over the table once more; her eyes had reached the word "Hessians"—it was to be stamped on her mind for life—when she heard a slight noise. Raising her eyes, they met D'Arcy's.

He was standing just inside the door; the candle, which he held high, lit up his handsome, puzzled face. Laughter and inquiry struggled in his eyes, as he saw the girl, draped in his huge cloak.

"Major D'Arcy!" she exclaimed.

"Miss Towneshend! I thought it was some lovely ghost," he said.

"I was never more in the flesh than I am to-night," she answered quietly, though her head was whirling again.

"Are you for a masquerade to-night,

187

Miss Towneshend?" asked D'Arcy, his eyes traveling once more over the slight, cloaked, girlish figure.

"I am," said Pamela, "and for a ride," she added, firmly.

"And may I accompany you?" he questioned. "It is a dark night."

Like a flash it had come over him that this girl, standing there defiant and at bay, was his enemy; had the information that would break their plans asunder, and would use it to the full.

"Thank you, Major D'Arcy," he heard her say, "but I must ride alone."

He was very grave now, the light had left his eyes; she felt that he had divined everything.

"I am afraid, Miss Towneshend, that I cannot permit you to leave this room alone to-night. Not for several hours, at least," he said.

"Do you mean that you would dare to use force to restrain me?" flashed out the girl, with blazing eyes.

"I should feel extremely mortified if you pushed me to that extremity," answered D'Arcy.

"Which means that you would?"

"Which means that I would." There was a coolness and deliberateness about the man that frenzied the girl, whose nerves were already a-tingle.

"The boasted chivalry of the Irish gentleman and the British officer fades away when put to the trial," she laughed.

"You do both the Irish gentleman, and the British officer, grave injustice, Miss Towneshend. You have in your possession information of the utmost importance to the enemy, which it is my duty to prevent from coming into their hands," he replied.

Swiftly the girl took another tack; there was pleading in her voice. "Let me go," she cried. "Can't you see — oh, let me go." She spoke eagerly and fast, her voice trembling, her cheeks on fire. He thought her the loveliest thing earth held and a mad impulse swept over him to take her in his arms, and give everything she asked. The next moment he felt stranded and sickened at the thought.

"You put me to a cruel test. If my love for you, Miss Towneshend, was one

189

whit less true or honest, I'd bid you go, and claim the reward of my dishonor. But I can't, I can't," he cried, desperately. "Give me your word that you will not leave this house to-night, or communicate to any other person the information which you possess, and I will not restrain you."

He took a step forward, and she felt as if her legs would give way; she leaned on the table, and her hand touched something. Involuntarily she grasped it; her hand closed around the handle familiarly. "No," she cried, "and Major D'Arcy," she added firmly, pulling back the trigger of the pistol, "you will prevent my passing at your peril."

He could see that she knew the weapon's use. "I would prefer it so," he replied, quite simply, and stepped toward her.

"I warn you!" cried Pamela, stepping back a pace and raising her arm.

"You cannot leave this room," he said, and his eye ran along the shining barrel in her hand. She saw the eye with a half smile in it, and lower down the firm, relentless mouth and she fired. He seemed to swing as if on a pivot, then, with a cry, pitched forward on the floor, the candlestick flying from his hand to a farther corner of the room.

Pamela stood dazed and stunned by the reverberation; the smoke drifted, and she saw him lying there, senseless—dead? With a cry she threw herself by his side, and raised his head. "He's dead; I've killed him," she said to Cynthia, who had entered silently, and knelt with her, horror-stricken.

"Quick, Pamela, you must go; Sambo has the mare at the back gate."

"Go!" gasped Pamela. "I can't leave him. Jack! Jack!" she moaned.

"There is some one coming," whispered Cynthia, hoarsely, staggering up, and pulling at Pamela. "Go, go, for Heaven's sake, or everything is lost." She half dragged the girl to her feet, across the room, and shoved her through the door. A second later, Gregory, his clothes all disordered, burst into the room.

"What is it? Who is hurt?"

"Major D'Arcy," said Cynthia.

Then he saw him lying there, sprawled

out, inanimate. Stooping quickly, he took him in his arms.

"Jack, Jack! My God, Jack, speak to me!" cried the old man, piteously.

But D'Arcy didn't answer.

CHAPTER XVI

PAMELA TAKES TO THE ROAD

Pamela groped her way along the hall, as if she were traversing the intricacies of some unfamiliar maze. Her feet were leaden, and every limb seemed in perverse revolt against her hideous retreat. She was possessed by the full horror of the thing, and every sense seemed numb. At the farther end a candle burned dimly, and, halting unsteadily for a moment, she snatched a fur tippet from the rack, and a hood, instinctively, with no mental prescience of the bitter night without. As she passed out, the frosty air gave her a stinging welcome, and the blood rushed to her paled cheeks; she felt revivified, and seeing the beams of Sambo's lantern sprinkling through the hedge, she hurried forward, will once more dominating. The old darky, snuggled closely in a great-coat, was coaxing the restive mare, in a low voice, when she appeared. He noticed

193

her bare hands, and forced his own huge
mittens on her; an instant later her leg
gripped the saddle-horn, and with a last
hurried, whispered message for Cynthia,
about her mother, she was off.

The road was an open book to her.
Every hollow, every hill, every side-lane
and by-path, belonged to her memory
from childhood; and there was no uncertainty in her mind when she turned into
the fields, after a racing mile that had set
the reluctant blood chasing through her,
and had communicated some of the mare's
buoyant mettle to her own jaded senses.
Her hand grew firmer on the rein, vision
came to her eyes, and most blessed of all,
that raging memory was subdued; the
night enveloped her and seemed to sub-
merge her tiny emotions and raw consciousness in its mighty infiniteness. The
precaution of taking to the frozen furrows
showed that her mind was alert, for, not a
quarter of a mile beyond, a small outpost
barred the road. Further on she took to
the main path again, and the mad gallop
was resumed. A blazing fire, with
shadowy figures about, far ahead, twisted

her aside once more, and she came out on the hillroad, the river twining blackly beneath her, and the journey nearly half over.

On and on they sped. Brown Bess, too, caught the spirit of the perilous adventure, and spurned the miles with every moment faster flying hoofs. Trees, with winter-blasted branches, seemed to beseech them to tarry, but on they hurried; grim, tight, shuttered houses, mocked at their haste, but they heeded not; the sluggish river rolled on, with its freight of grinding ice, and showed no interest in the race, while the twinkling stars, only, speeded them on cheerily. Even the comfort they yielded, was denied, when they entered the jealous blackness of a wood, where only dimmest shadows kept them company, and stealthy midnight noises met their approach and again sounded in their rear. At last, they left the open for good, and were embraced by the impenetrable gloom of the forest. The mare was reined in to an impatient and fretful walk, while the girl leaned forward, and peered into the darkness.

There was no sound save Bess's iron stamp on the frozen ground, and for a mile or more they walked, then, of a sudden, a shrill whistle split the air in front of them. Pamela heard the breaking of twigs and the rustle of bushes; with tight-held breath, she waited, the mare curbed in firmly; they must be friends there, she felt, and took the chance.

A muffled group was soon about her, and hands held the bridle. She could distinguish neither face nor uniform, but she saw bayonets, and knew they were soldiery, and their voices proclaimed them friends. As for the picket, when they discovered the cloaked figure to be a girl, and heard that her errand was to headquarters, vigilance gave way to courtesy, and she was hurried on, with a guard of honor, to her journey's end.

The hour was one, and the camp slept as they passed among its numberless rows of tents and huts; fires burned brightly, here and there, and guardian sentries questioned their approach, only to give way before the whispered countersign. At last, they halted before the door of a log house larger than those they had passed, and with tell-tale rays of light stealing from behind closely-curtained windows, to show that the inmates were not abed. A sounding rap brought the door open, and there were whisperings with the guard. Then the portal was closed, and they all stood silent; the girl shivering above them, while the mare, with steaming flanks, pounded restlessly. The door was flung wide again, after an interminable wait, and a man stepped toward her, his sword and spurs clanking as he walked. He stood beside her, and spoke, and she reeled in the saddle.

"Ned!" she cried, and he had her in his arms.

She was conscious of being borne tenderly into the warmth of a lighted room, then all was blank. When she came to, her brother was kneeling at her side, gently chafing the frosted hands, and another, she thought the biggest man she had ever seen, was standing by. He spoke gently, in a low voice, and in answer she heard her brother call him

"General." Then thought came with a rush; she sat up quickly.

"What is the hour?" she asked.

"After one," answered Ned. "Have you news?" he said.

"News?" she burst out. "They are starting now!"

"They?" cried her brother.

"The British," she answered, and followed with the tale, but with no mention of that sprawling figure on the floor of the book-room; she had shoved the picture of that into the furthest corner of her memory, and now, breathlessly, told only of the plan. The tall man hung on every word, his eyes bent on her in grave scrutiny. By the time she had finished, he had stepped quickly to a table littered with papers, and taking a quill, wrote rapidly, turning once to question her. Then Ned hurriedly left the room.

The big man once more stood by her; he seemed to tower in his height, and she noticed the great size of his hands, and booted feet, while wonder possessed her at his gentleness. He spoke of finding her comfortable accommodations for the night, but she begged him the privilege of sitting by the fire, there; the night had a thousand terrors for her, that had sprung to life since her brother's strong arms had held her, and she knew she could not stand the strain of a strange, lonely room and bed. The General yielded, gently, as he would to a child, and soothed her. Before many moments had passed, Ned was back, with several others, who looked curiously at the girl, but who were soon listening intently to the quick, low voice of the General. Ned was once more by her side, as they talked, holding her hand, speaking tenderly.

"Who is he?" she asked, with eyes directed to the tall, blue-coated figure.

"The General," answered Ned.

"What General?" she asked.

"Washington," he whispered, and turned from her, as his own name was called.

The hum of voices, and the heat of the fire, drowsed her, and she dozed off, not waking even at the far-off roll of drums, that sounded. Indeed, heart and brain-weary as she was, it was not till late that

199

she awoke; then the crash of musketry
roused her sluggard senses, and the deep-
toned roar of artillery brought her to her
feet, wide-eyed. She stumbled to the
window, but it was still black without;
once, in a brief interval of silence, she
heard shouts, to be followed once more by
the dreadful crash and roar, a fearful
cacophony, that seemed to split the night
in twain. She huddled once more before
the dying embers, and drew the cloak
tightly about her. His cloak, she thought,
with a shudder; and memory, pried open
once more, spread before her mind's eye
the horrid scene: the red coat, spattered
with life's red, the pale face, the clenched
hands—oh, the horror of it! She could
have screamed in terror, but the hideous
noise overpowered her; it seemed growing
faster, louder, nearer. She did scream,
but no sound came, and again: then life
seemed to drop away from her, and she
was still.

She was lying outstretched on a skin-
covered pallet, when her eyes opened next.
She could hear the crackling of a freshly-
piled fire, and the cold, gray light of the

early winter morning, drifting through the frosted panes, showed her brother, standing by the hissing logs. She spoke weakly, and he sprang to her side, his blackened face lit joyously.

"We've won!" he cried.

"Won?" she said, weakly.

"Driven 'em back, with hundreds dead and prisoners." His voice was full of high elation, and his bloodshot eyes still gleamed with the battle fever. "And it's all your doing, sis, dear; all your doing."

The color mounted slowly to her cheeks, but she had no feeling of joy. What of it? she thought, and smarting memory dragged her back a thousand years, it seemed; but still terribly, horribly vivid.

The big General entered soon after, and her blood did quicken at his words. "Mistress Towneshend," he said, "we have good cause to be thankful to the Towneshend family this morning. Your pluck has saved us from a great calamity, and your brother has performed prodigies." He placed his hand on the young man's shoulder, and she could see Ned blushing

201

furiously. He spoke further, but her interest faded.

They breakfasted together, but she was silent, only intent on the hour when she should start on the backward journey. No persuasion would keep her in the camp another night, and, shortly after dusk, with a small escort of troopers, and her brother at her side, she set out. It was different from the mad scamper of the night before; they took other roads, and felt their way cautiously. The distance seemed interminable, and Pamela wondered, dreamily, how she and Bess had covered it—and lived. The escort halted about three miles from the town and waited, while Towneshend went forward with her alone. Then he, too, turned back, after' a thousand dear messages to the loved ones, and a kiss, which she received passively. She had been like stone the whole day, and had bewildered and frightened her brother. He was reassured, however, by the vehemence with which she had urged her home-going, but his misgivings rose again, as he was about to leave her.

"I am well, Ned," she said; "don't worry."

But he did, and watched her canter away out of sight, fearfully.

She reached the house without further adventure, and a low, discreet whistle brought the devoted Sambo, lantern in hand, hurrying out. He was bursting with a hundred questions, but she brushed his loquacity aside, and fairly ran for the house. The back door was open, and she passed through hurriedly, and to the little sitting-room frequented at night by Cynthia and herself.

"Pamela!" exclaimed her cousin, as she stood before her, and they were locked in one another's arms.

"He is—is dead?" stammered Pamela, holding her hard at arm's length.

"No," answered her cousin.

"Thank God," she said, fervently.

"He is still unconscious," said Cynthia, "but Dr. Gregory has every hope. Tell me everything."

"I know nothing," cried Pamela. "I must go to him."

And, a little later, in answer to a timid

knock, Gregory opened to her, and she stood before him, haggard, pale, and wild-eyed.

"I can help you," she said, pleadingly.

"Not with those rings about your pretty eyes, dear," the old man answered, gently. "Rest to-night, and to-morrow we'll see."

She could have wept, pride was so little a part of her now; but she stifled back the sobs and crept off to bed, praying for the day.

CHAPTER XVII

COMPENSATIONS

The three weeks that followed were trying ones for all three. To D'Arcy, lying stretched, with a shattered arm, and torn side, from which the bullet had been extracted; to Gregory, constant and indefatigable in attention, and to the silent, hovering girl. There were desperate moments of pain for all; then long, still watches, with moaning intervals, while nature grappled with the wounded man, and bore him on, at snail's pace, out of the shadow.

Side by side, the old Doctor and Pamela waited with their hearts in their mouths. The little tragedy had come to Gregory like a bolt from a clear sky, and though he was too old a campaigner to lose his wits, it had stunned and unnerved him. The lad was the center of his little universe, and to see him laid low, shut the light out of his life. He was completely

in the dark, too, as to the happening, and
that worried him. For a wild moment,
that night, he had thought of Dacier, but
common sense and later reports dispelled
that. Cynthia had told him of hearing
the shot, and rushing in to find D'Arcy
on the floor. He could get nothing else
from her. Was there anything else to
get? He didn't know. D'Arcy himself
could not speak, and he had finally to
give up surmise and wait. Cynthia told
him, further, that her cousin was ill, and
her appearance the next night, tapping at
the door, bore this out. Indeed, it was
only the girl's resistless supplication that
gained her admittance. He was afraid of
having two invalids on his hands. But he
became accustomed, after a day or so, to
the quiet, tireless figure, that glided
noiselessly in and out on sick-room
errands, and after a fortnight she had
made herself indispensable to him, and the
wounded Guardsman, too.

D'Arcy watched her for days, as if in a
dream. Then, summoning courage, he
questioned Gregory, and the color came
and went in his pale cheeks when he was

told that Pamela had been waiting on him day and night. He said nothing, but there was no pleasure in his thoughts. They were alone in the room, at times, for hours, he pretending the deepest sleep, while often in an agony for water, a change of position, or one of the hundred of a sick man's needs. Anything could be borne but her pitying ministrations; and still, the room seemed bare, uncomfortable, and colorless to him when it lacked her presence.

Never had she seemed so near and familiar to him, and yet separated by such immeasurable distances. As the days dragged on, this far-away familiarity grew into a tantalizing but dear intimacy. Through half-closed lids, when she was unaware, he studied and doted on every line and bend of her supple figure, watched her quick, simple movements, her mass of brown hair,—sometimes wayward and astray, but oftener cabined by the daintiest of caps,—and, once or thrice, she set his heart pumping by a flash of eyes. And this woman, the woman of all women for him, who had scorned his love, who, when he had stood in her path, had stricken him down wrathfully, now succored and tenderly served him. "Through what?" he asked himself, a hundred times, to receive but the one answer, that always set him writhing: "Pity!" Such was the value of the young gentleman's worldly experience.

And through the weary days, Pamela was battling, too. She had mighty fortifications of pride and maidenly reserve, but gradually they were reduced, one after another, by the steady, persistent onslaughts of remorse, and that subtle engine of siege: love. Capitulation was delayed time and again, but at last complete surrender came in confession to herself: the hardest task; and once the humiliation of it was tasted to the full, she winged to heights that dropped the world dizzily beneath, and a beatified, tremulous content was hers; a content that turned to torment, however, ere she had fairly grasped it. She fell a victim to the inexorable law of compensation, and the hapless D'Arcy, all unconsciously, was avenged.

It fell out in a simple way, and was the cause of long days and nights of delicious agony. The fourth week of the young Irishman's bed-ridden existence was drifting by, when one morning Pamela noticed for the first time, on his dressing-table, a tiny, exquisite miniature. It was conspicuous enough in its tarnished, gilded frame, among the table's load of silver, but it had never caught her eye before. She took it in her hand, curiously, with no misgiving, and from that moment, content was banished, and her heart ached dully for many a long day. Never, she thought, had she seen so beautiful a face as that delicately painted one, which looked at her quite frankly, with great, winsome blue eyes; the hair was high, in puffy rolls, powdered, and with a white plume; the gleam of neck, through fur, was a further beauty; the whole effect ravishing, and she put the picture down, a jealous woman. If she took it up once during the day, she took it up fifty times, and that was the torture of the succeeding days. At nights she dreamed of it, and waking, the merry eyes and smiling lips

mocked her every moment. It became a
dreadful, hateful nemesis, and she loathed
it, though it had a compelling fascination.
She knew Gregory could enlighten her,
but she shrank from asking, though the
question trembled on her lips a dozen
times. Tantalizing ignorance was better
than a knowledge that might mean, she
dreaded to think what.

And so the two self-tortured young
people passed through a grim five weeks;
neither one guessing the other's secret;
and both oblivious to the fact that one
other possessed both. Gregory, with the
aid of his solitary evening pipes, and the
previous knowledge he had of D'Arcy's
condition, had caught the drift of affairs,
and dreaded the coming convalescence,
which was at hand. In fact, it came
sooner than he had dared to hope, and his
patient was soon clamoring to be let upon
his feet.

It was a bitter day, near the end of
February, when that notable event at
last took place. Very pale and very
weak, wrapped in his gorgeous dressing-
gown—on which his arm, slung in black

silk, rested like a blot—and leaning heavily on his old friend, he shuffled into the big, bright, cosy sitting-room, where a huge fire crackled a welcome to him, and the sunbeams danced merrily at his approach. He was as irritable as an old cat, but Gregory bore with him gently, in fact rather liked it as a sign of returning spirits.

"Damn it, Greg, don't be so careful; I'm not going to break," he growled.

"Sit here, by the fire, boy," answered the old man, letting him drop gently into a great chair that was placed directly in front of the blaze. "Some one has evidently prepared against your coming," he added, with a twinkle, and pushing the footstool a trifle nearer.

"Oh, you and she both coddle me like a child," said D'Arcy. "I won't have it, Greg," he flung out, angrily.

"Tell Miss Towneshend that yourself," rejoined Gregory. "It will be a very gracious way of thanking her for her services. And I, myself, will trouble no more about you," added the old man, huffily.

"I'm a beast, Greg; forgive me," answered the youngster, "but it's hard, damned hard."

"Of course, it's hard, lad, but we've pulled you through," said the other, gently.

"Yes, you've pulled me through, but I'd rather have stopped at the other end. You know, I'll never use it again," said D'Arcy, piteously, pointing to the arm that hung helpless.

"You want to be thankful I didn't take it off," answered the doctor, forcing his gaiety.

"I don't want to be, and I'm not. To think that that good right hand that has served me so well," he went on, "will never grasp sword-hilt or press trigger again. But I'll shoot with the left, Greg, and will show him a rapier can be handled well enough on the other side."

"Show who?" exclaimed Gregory, wondering if the lad had gone out of his head. "What are you talking about, man?"

"That blackguard, Dacier," answered D'Arcy. "You remember that night, he dared to speak of her."

"Surely I told you, Jack," said the old man, gently.

"Told me what?"

"About Dacier."

"You told me nothing."

"He was killed in the first charge that awful morning."

"Killed!" cried D'Arcy.

"And Farquhar, too," added the doctor.

"Poor boys," said the Irishman, his head drooping. "God rest their souls."

This was the first of many similar mornings, and patient, doctor and nurse left the sick-room behind with gay hearts. The sunny sitting-room, where they now foregathered, warmed them all, after the chill days of fever and worry. Pamela was still haunted miserably by the laughing face of a gracious dame in high, powdered coiffure, and D'Arcy bore a gnawing pain that was not in his arm, while old Gregory watched, waited, and felt for them both.

CHAPTER XVIII

The old Quaker town held high revel.
Gaming, feasting, and dancing appealed
more to the doughty Sir William Howe,
than winter campaigning, and annihilation
of the enemy was postponed till spring.
There were a few who fretted at the dalli-
ance, but it was a gay little army of occupation, and dull care and mordant
memories fled before their festivities.
The galling disappointment of their sharp
repulse at Valley Forge was the talk for
nine days, of mess-room and barracks, but
it was an optimistic little army, too, and
not easily ruffled. The end of the
rebellion, in their minds, was simply postponed till the frost had left the ground,
then horrid retribution was to follow swiftly
on their path, and His Majesty's enemies
were to be smitten from the earth's face.

The news of their favorite's recovery
spread through the town, and not a day

215

passed but D'Arcy held a small levee. Young officers and old crowded his sunny sitting-room, and only left when the watchful Gregory turned them out; Sir William and the Earl of Cornwallis, too, called and congratulated him on his convalescence. There were many questionings as to the cause of his accident, but no suspicion was aroused by his vague tale of a pistol's careless handling. Only his lynx-eyed old friend thought that there were things left untold. It was late one winter's afternoon, when they were sitting together alone in the dusk, that the old man, for the first time, ventured to probe into the mystery.

"Tell me, Jack," he said, "how did it happen? You've never given any decent account of it."

"I have no decent account to give," answered D'Arcy, leaning forward with tongs, to lift a recalcitrant log into the blaze. "I stopped at the gate to talk with Dalrymple for a moment, and then came back to the house."

"Yes," interrupted Gregory, quickly, "and you found her there?"

"I found no one there," replied the Irishman, not turning a hair.

"Oh, I thought you did," said Gregory, puffing clouds, and seeing that it was no easy matter to get through his friend's guard. "Go on," he added.

"Well, I walked over to the table," went on D'Arcy, deliberately, settling back in his chair, "put down the candle, and picked up one of the pistols. And somehow or other, the damned thing went off."

"Did you pick it up with your left hand?" questioned the doctor, quietly.

"How the devil do I know which hand I picked it up with?" answered the young man, pettishly, having recourse to the tongs again.

"That's what I would like to know," replied Gregory, drily. "How the devil could you know?"

"I picked it up with my right hand," snapped out D'Arcy, getting angry.

"And it went off?" said the old man.

"That's what I said."

"Then how did it happen to hit you in the right arm and side?" There was too much of the pride of the successful cross-examiner in Gregory's voice, and D'Arcy turned on him, furiously.

"I will not be cross-examined and bullied, Greg," he cried. "It's unkind of you. I tell you, it went off, and that's all I know about it."

Fortunately, at that moment came a familiar tap at the door, and Gregory opened it to Pamela. D'Arcy tried eagerly to rise, but she motioned him not.

"You must not move, Major," she said. "I've brought you your broth." She handed him a snowy napkin, and the steaming, savory bowl.

"Thanks," he said. "You take too much trouble for a well man. I am getting quite myself."

"He'll soon be defying us both, Doctor," she answered, gaily, turning to Gregory.

"Yes, he'd dispense with us now, if he could," grunted Gregory, and then, seized by some perverse inspiration, he added, "He has just been telling me how the accident happened."

Luckily for the girl, the friendly dusk

shadowed her paled cheeks and involuntary start, and there was no sign of trepidation in her cool, "Indeed?"

"Yes," went on the doctor, "and I can't, for the life of me, see how he did it, unless he was trying to commit suicide," he added, jocosely.

She had herself well in hand now, and replied in the same mood, "The Major is too good a shot to have bungled it, if that was what he was trying to do."

"For heaven's sake, Greg, shut up," interposed D'Arcy. "Miss Towneshend has had trials enough the last five or six weeks, without being bothered further about the stupid business."

"I'm mum," rejoined the doctor.

And a few moments later Pamela departed, tremblingly, thankful for D'Arcy's interposition.

"She's a goddess, Greg," murmured the youngster, as the door closed behind her.

"I beg to differ with you, Jack," said the old man, seating himself again. "I think she's human, and very much of a woman."

"Ah, you old misogynist! What do you

know about the sex, and what do you care?'' laughed D'Arcy.

''I know more about this particular young lady than you may imagine.''

''And, pray, what do you know?''

''That she's very much in love with a friend of mine, named Jack D'Arcy.''

''Are you mocking me, Greg, or are you mad?'' cried the Irishman, springing to his feet, and turning on the old man.

''Neither, may it please your worship.''

''I thought you'd have had more sense than to have imagined such a thing.''

''Why has the young person been fluttering about you for the past two months, if she hasn't designs on you?'' asked Gregory, coolly.

''It's pity, Greg, pity,'' said the other, bitterly, and then he added, stiffly, ''Please don't speak of her to me as a young person.''

''A thousand pardons. And what is it they say pity is akin to?''

D'Arcy turned a pitiable face to him. ''Don't, Greg, don't,'' he cried, ''I can't bear it. Can't you see it's breaking my heart, man. She gives me pity and tenderness, as she'd give it to a child, or some other broken, worthless thing, such as I. But her love! She'll keep that for a man; a man who can guard and shield her with his good right arm."

All the pent-up anguish in the man's heart burst forth in this little speech, and brought tears to the old man's eyes.

"God forbid, Jack," he said, "that I should ever think the calumny you breathe against her."

"It's no calumny," cried D'Arcy. "Do you think any blame attaches to her? Do you think I snivel because, angel that she is, she doesn't see fit to fall in love with a piece of a man?"

"I think you're working yourself into a very harmful state of excitement, that's what I think. Sit down." He was alarmed at the other's quiet intensity.

"Curse it, Greg," went on the young man, "would you have me take it like a stone image? I shall sail for England as soon as I'm able to put foot aboard ship, and what has life for me there? It'll be ashes in my mouth."

"And all because you were careless in

handling a pistol," Gregory couldn't help saying. D'Arcy made no answer, but turned savagely on the fire. The old man watched him silently for a few moments, then spoke again. "See here, Jack, what's the use of ruining your happiness for the sake of an idea?" he asked.

"Don't talk like a philosophical treatise," was the rejoinder. "What do you mean?"

"I mean that your beastly pride has choked the common sense out of you. Give the girl a chance."

"Would you have me crawl to her like a crippled beggar, and try to work on her sympathies?" sneered D'Arcy.

"Perhaps your potential lordship would prefer to have the lady make the advances," was the reply.

"Greg, you'll drive me mad with your folly. What have I to give her? How on earth could I dare to hope to make her happy? I'm a wreck of a man, and no fit mate for her likes."

"Nonsense," said the old man, bound to make his impression. "You'll be as strong as ever you were, in a month.

And as for what you have to give her, a pretty estate and an old name are not to be snuffed at, even by a little American rebel. There is many a London dame who would jump at the chance of being My Lady D'Arcy.''

"I can't agree with you, Greg, and what you suggest is impossible. You don't understand women as I do, old man, and, therefore, there is no use of talking about it further.'' There was the note of finality in his voice, and Gregory drew off from the attack.

"As you please, Jack,'' he acquiesced, and withdrew his forces in good order, with full determination to renew the attack in another quarter.

Opportunity was shy for a day or two, during which time D'Arcy talked constantly of his immediate return to England. The old man knew that it would be impossible to detain him much longer, and he was resolved to appeal to Pamela. He chanced upon her quite by accident, one morning on his way out, in the book-room, and decided to speak plainly at once.

"Miss Towneshend," he said, "I want to speak with you about Major D'Arcy."

"He is not so well?" she asked, anxiously, the color mounting in her cheeks.

"He is not well at all," went on Gregory, bluntly, "and next week he proposes to sail for England."

"For England?" she faltered, blankly. "He is going back—you think him unable to stand the voyage?"

"Under certain conditions it would do him good," answered the doctor, fully conscious that he had filled the girl with consternation.

"And will he not go under the most favorable conditions?"

"That depends entirely upon you, Miss Towneshend," he replied, deliberately.

"Upon me? I don't understand."

"Miss Towneshend," said the old man, gently enough, "women can wound in more ways than one; and a bullet wound is not necessarily the most dangerous thing that can befall a man."

"You are talking riddles," stammered Pamela, faintly.

"I will speak plainly," he said. "Jack

D'Arcy has entirely recovered fromt he ill effects of his shattered arm, but a very dangerous malady has him in its clutches."

"What?" she cried.

"Love-sickness," answered Gregory.

"Captain Gregory, are you trying to make merry at my expense?"

"Nothing could be further from my thought, Miss Towneshend," he said, kindly. "I speak only because Jack D'Arcy's happiness is a dear thing to me. I have known him, as lad and man, these twenty years, and I can't stand by to see his life broken simply on account of a misunderstanding."

"A misunderstanding?" she quavered.

"Just that. The man is mad in love with you, and has been, ever since the first day he set foot in your gardens, yonder."

She smiled sadly, tolerantly, at the old man's folly. "Captain Gregory," she said, "you speak from the heart, I know; out of the fullness of your wish for your friend's happiness. But you are utterly mistaken in your idea. He does not love me; he despises me." These words were flung from her, with a vehemence that startled him.

"Despise you!" he cried. "Miss Towneshend, are you in your right senses?"

"Ah, you can't mislead a woman in such a matter," she replied, more quietly. "Major D'Arcy may have had a passing fancy—once; but you don't know all, you don't know all. He can never love me." There were tears in her voice, but they made no impression on the old man, who was simply irritated.

"I tell you, I know what I'm talking about," he said.

"Did he send you to me?" she asked.

"No," Gregory replied, eagerly. "He said there was no use."

"And he was right."

"Don't you care for him?" spluttered the doctor, fast losing self-control, "for, if you don't, I'm an old simpleton."

"I have made no pretense of not caring for him," said Pamela, in a low voice, with down-bent eyes.

"And yet the young fool says it's only sympathy. Bah!" ejaculated the old man.

"He has a chivalrous regard for my feelings," she answered.

"My dear young lady, can't you see?" he questioned, testily. The perversity of the two was slowly, but surely, delivering him into the hands of his temper. Her answer was almost all that was needed.

"We women do not see in such matters. We feel," she said. "A woman's heart tells truth."

"Rubbish! Miss Towneshend, pure rubbish. You've been reading too much of Mr. Richardson," he retorted.

She saw that he was mightily put out and annoyed, and she offered him her hand. "Captain Gregory," she said, "you've been very kind, but I am afraid your wishes father your thoughts. I thank you from the bottom of my heart, but I know it can never be."

He hardly heard her; he only knew that a malign waywardness seemed to possess these young people, and that they were determined to shut the door on their own happiness. It was unbearable, and choler at last bested him.

"I will not stay here to be so abominably

227

misunderstood," he cried. "You are both a pair of blind young idiots, and I wash my hands of the whole thing."

He swung his cloak about him violently and made for the door, poor Pamela standing amazed. He turned before leaving, and was about to speak, but thinking better of it, bowed and made exit; his muttered "Oh, damn!" floating back behind him.

The girl was all of a tremble and would have dissolved, if it had not been for the memory of a pair of dancing eyes and cherry lips, that smiled at her from a gilded frame,—her unknown rival.

CHAPTER XIX

ADJUSTMENTS

D'Arcy's talk about returning to England soon developed into preparation. He was daily getting stronger, and would soon be able to stand the journey to New York, where he intended to take passage aboard a frigate that was to sail about the first of March. Gregory kept close-mouthed, and had a painful satisfaction in knowing the punishment that Chance was meting out to two who would not see, but this selfsame Chance was capable of vagaries that even he was unsuspicious of. It decreed pale cheeks and lusterless eyes to the young Irishman, and a broken spirit to the maid, then whirled inconsequently about, and uplifted them both.

It was a day of queer happenings in the "next week," that had been the burden of D'Arcy's talk of departure. Reports of the preparations had reached Pamela, through Sambo, and she braced herself stoically, though drooping within. The day of broths and special little culinary preparations for the invalid had long since passed, and they seldom met. She wondered if he would say good-bye; the word sounded like a knell, and she could have prayed to be spared the hearing of it from his lips. But she must see him before he went; that was imperative. He had made no allusion to that terrible night, but she could never rest with the burden of it till she had pleaded for pardon; that little he might afford to give.

She arose on the eventful morning, wretchedly wan and tired. Breakfast was an unwelcome obligation, and even Cynthia, who was growing accustomed to a dejected and spiritless Pamela, could not refrain from comment. It passed unheeded, and only the startling appearance of Sambo, with bulging eyes, drove away the listlessness.

"Massa Ned's come!"

"Who?" she cried, springing up.

"Are you mad, Sambo?" gasped Cynthia.

But his wits were approved that instant by the entrance of the tall young dragoon, who bent a moment later under a loving weight.

They pelted him with a hundred questions, and wondered at his dress in full uniform. He joked, and teased them gaily; said that he had come to attack the British single-handed, and much more foolishness to the same effect, but finally told them that he was in under a flag of truce, to negotiate an exchange of prisoners. The moments were precious, and Pamela sped to her mother, to give warning of his approach, in which was mixed a tender thoughtfulness for the lovers.

Was it Chance that took her through the book-room? Who can tell? She might have gone the other way around, but didn't; and as she crossed the threshold, she saw him standing before the fire. He was dressed in black, and though his face was as white as the lace at his wrists and neck, he had never seemed so handsome. His arm hung in a scarlet sling, the one touch of color. Her first instinct was to withdraw, but he had turned and faced her before she could follow it out.

"Miss Towneshend," he said, "I have been wishing for just this opportunity. I want to speak to you."

She felt that the "good-bye" was coming, and her tongue clove to her mouth; she was icy cold.

"I can't thank you in words for all you've done for me these last weeks," he added.

"Don't, Major D'Arcy," cried the girl, painfully. "Don't thank me. Forgive me, if you can, in your heart; but to thank me for what little reparation I have been able to make stings like a blow."

He looked at her, in wonder.

"Forgive you, Miss Towneshend. And you speak of reparation? It was the fortune of war; I abide by it, and," he said, gently, the old light coming into his eyes, "I shall always hold as my sweetest memory the recollection of my lovely opponent."

"You are magnanimous," was all she could say.

232

"Magnanimity is a poor gift, from one who is beaten," he answered, quietly.

"I didn't mean that, believe me, Major D'Arcy," she replied, eagerly. "And if I could do anything, oh, anything, to atone for the cowardly advantage I took of you that night——"

"Pray don't distress yourself, Miss Towneshend. All is fair in—in war," he stammered, shrinking from the pit that dreadful other word would have opened before him. "The war-god had his choice between us, and he would have been a churl to have chosen otherwise than as he did."

"You insist on making light of my offense," she said.

"The offense, if any, was condoned by the pluck and loyalty that prompted it," spoke the soldier.

"You are too generous a foe, Major D'Arcy."

"My reward is in your saying it. It will be some comfort, when I am gone, to know that one 'red-coat' lies gently in your thought."

"Captain Gregory was right—you are going soon?"

"Yes, I leave to-morrow."

"I—we shall—miss you," said poor Pamela, hardly above a whisper. Something in that whisper brought him a step nearer. Their eyes met steadily, then hers dropped.

"You will care?" he asked, and hung on her answer.

"I care more than—than I dare to tell," she answered, and he was at her side, taking her unresisting hand.

"Pamela! It can't be true!" he burst out—"Greg can't be right."

"What did he say?" she asked, a tremor of hope and fear shaking her.

"That you — you loved me. Oh, no, no, no, he couldn't see what I didn't."

"But he did," said Pamela humbly, and then a great wave of feeling surged through her. This might be her last moment with him. He should know all; she would give him the opportunity to spurn her; that would be her punishment.

"I love you," she cried, "and I—I can't stand your going away." She waited for the blow, but his arm was about her, and his kisses were on her cheeks.

"Oh, it can't be true," she gasped. "Captain Gregory can't be right."

"What did he say?" asked D'Arcy, radiant.

"That you loved me still," she answered.

"He never spoke truer word. I love you, Pamela, heart and soul."

"But the other," she faltered, unable to believe.

"What other?"

"The miniature."

"What miniature?"

"On your dressing-table. I—I hate her," said Pamela.

"Oh," laughed the Irishman, his eyes sparkling. "Never, you must love her; she's my mother!"

Some moments later, she said: "You do forgive me?"

"Hush!" he replied. "Are you sure you don't pity me?"

"Pity you? For what?"

"For being beaten."

"But you've won," said Pamela. "You've conquered the rebel."

"Faith, and so I have," replied D'Arcy. "You're my prisoner."

"For life," said the girl, fondly. And Gregory found them together when he came in later.

D'Arcy was quite brazen, and reassured the startled girl, nonchalantly: "It's only Greg, Pamela."

"Oh, it's only Greg, is it?" said the grizzled old giant, looking from one to the other, in blank amazement.

"May I call you Greg, too?" asked Pamela, stepping to him, timidly.

"You may call him anything you please, dear. But I call him an old scoundrel," said D'Arcy. "You dear old rascal, you know more of the sex than I ever suspected."

"Oho," laughed the doctor, "so the two young fools have gotten their eyes open, eh? I congratulate you, Major D'Arcy, and you, Miss Towneshend——"

"Pamela, please," she interposed.

"Pamela, my dear," corrected the old man. "Did he crawl to you like a

236

crippled beggar; did the fine gentleman pocket his pride, and allow the angel to shine upon him?"

"Oh, shut up," cried the Irishman.

"And, Pamela, do you think women's hearts always tell 'em the truth?"

"What are you talking about?" asked the puzzled D'Arcy.

"He's being very silly," said Pamela, blushing furiously.

"Old Greg is not such a fool as he looks, eh?"

"You're the dearest old Greg in the world," said D'Arcy, and just then there was further interruption, caused by the entrance of Cynthia and Towneshend, who stared in wonderment.

Pamela darted to Cynthia and kissed her, exclaiming, "Oh, Cynthia, something has happened." She needed to speak no further. D'Arcy was introducing Gregory to the younger officer.

"I am glad to hear that you are convalescing, Major," said Towneshend.

"Yes, Gregory here and your sister have made a new man of me. You are exchanging prisoners?" asked D'Arcy.

"Yes," said Towneshend, smiling. "A little different from my last visit."

"Well, Captain," said the Irishman, with his old-time twinkle, "there is one prisoner that cannot be exchanged."

"Indeed?" was the mystified reply.

"Yes," said D'Arcy, stepping toward Pamela, and lightly taking her hand, "the fortunes of war have made your sister a prisoner for life, eh, Pamela?"

"It's so, Ned," she answered, simply, through a mist of tears. "For Life."

THE END

www.ingramcontent.com/pod-product-compliance
Lightning Source LLC
Chambersburg PA
CBHW031953060726
47497CB00016B/1994